T0128250

RELAXATION STORIES
— FOR —
SHARING
WITH OTHERS

An Anthology of Stories
Based on Life Events and a Fanciful Mind
Adding to Your Reading Pleasure

Bill Pechumer

authorHOUSE®

AuthorHouse™
1663 Liberty Drive
Bloomington, IN 47403
www.authorhouse.com
Phone: 1 (800) 839-8640

Published by AuthorHouse 04/20/2016

ISBN: 978-1-5049-6427-2 (sc)
ISBN: 978-1-5049-6425-8 (hc)
ISBN: 978-1-5049-6426-5 (e)

Library of Congress Control Number: 2016906693

Print information available on the last page.

Any people depicted in stock imagery provided by Thinkstock are models,
and such images are being used for illustrative purposes only.
Certain stock imagery © Thinkstock.

This book is printed on acid-free paper.

Because of the dynamic nature of the Internet, any web addresses or links contained in
this book may have changed since publication and may no longer be valid. The views
expressed in this work are solely those of the author and do not necessarily reflect the
views of the publisher, and the publisher hereby disclaims any responsibility for them.

No patent liability is assumed with respect to the use of information contained herein.

Although every precaution has been taken in the preparation of this publication,
the author assumes no responsibility for errors or omissions. Neither is any liability
assumed for damages resulting from the use of the information contained herein.

For information regarding permissions, write to Bill Pechumer,
18621 Amanda Lane, Hagerstown, MD, 21742.

"Crying on the Field" and "Mother Mary Ann Dressed in Calico" are historical fiction
stories. Characters may be real or fictional; the situations are based on fact.

All other stories in this anthology representing people and places are fictional, and
any resemblance to actual places or persons living or dead is coincidental.

Contents

Crying on the Field 1

Nosy Billy 33

UFOs Are Martians on Earth 36

Crackers 50

American Dating Blunders 54

Mother Mary Ann Dressed in Calico 66

Dare...99

A Modern Love Story..109

Time Stood Still..143

A Left Foot...151

Senior Citizen Art of Camping.................................155

About the Author 163

Crying on the Field

Many, many teardrops and souls fell during the American Civil War on the Antietam battlefield. After a costly battle during which 60 percent of Brigadier General John Bell Hood's forces became casualties, an officer asked him where his division was. Looking down and somber but resolute in his desire to tell the truth, the general was laconic.

—Dead on the field.

When I was young, I was troubled by all the talk and threats of a civil war and by the raids conducted by John Brown of Chambersburg, Pennsylvania. The exchange of opinions at the farm mill were very unsettling. I was a blacksmith apprentice, and my mind was not on fighting but on gaining a skill and marrying my girl, Bette. We wanted a life in a city, one with no worries, but the constant arguing in Congress and the endless frustration kept me confused. My feelings were as troubled as any farmer's opinion.

I was born in 1839 and raised in Greencastle, Pennsylvania. Our farm family included my father, Harold, my mother, Vera, two sisters— Mary and Gail—and brothers Amos and Daniel. Our family knew our role in life was growing corn. I'm muscular with broad shoulders and won many wrasslin' matches on the July 4th holidays.

As was the norm, my schooling stopped with sixth grade. I wanted to become a blacksmith. Having only seen boys fighting, the idea of war was beyond my thinking. The word *war* to me just meant people playing poker and somebody not being able to cover his bet. Other than some shoving and fisticuffs, nothing bad.

The states' conflict was often the talk at the dinner table. My parents tried to tone down my brothers' and sisters' dialogue about it but occasionally became involved in it themselves. We agreed slavery was wrong. A person could work as a servant or work to pay off a debt, but slavery involved people being bought and sold, traded, or given to another by a supposed owner.

—Bret, you're quiet tonight. Got a piece to say? my father asked.

—I was just thinking, I replied.

Their eyes focused on me. Forks fell onto plates. Me thinking and then speaking was like the full moon appearing twice in a month. I often joked when speaking.

—If I got a trip to Harrisburg with Mr. Butler and just looked at the farms on the way, do I owe him service? I asked.

—Did you help him with chores in Harrisburg? Amos asked.

—Sure. Why else would I have ridden?

—The chores were the service, as you call it, Amos said. You owe him nothing. You did something.

—Oh. I paused. Why do people need to have slaves?

—There are people in the world always wanting to take advantage of others. We often don't realize it until after it has started, my mother said reflectively.

A dessert dish was passed. The talk shifted to Bessie, the family cow, being in the family way and due any day.

I am a curious but quiet person, always thinking about things like the stars' patterns and the moon. I wondered what it would be like to live on the moon and look at the blue planet circling us. How much I didn't know!

I had learned in school what happened in wars; heroes in combat, spies getting caught, and the escapes of Paul Revere and "Light Horse" Harry or Ann Bates.

I learned to read lips. I watched other people's expressions and postures and such; that was fascinating. The body, especially the hands, expresses what is about to be said. Someone about to yell will open his mouth wide or give a quizzical look with the eyebrows. Eyes staring elsewhere are lying. I also learned to walk in different styles, lamely or quietly, on tiptoe. The Robinson Crusoe book was a revelation.

Over the border from Maryland by just two miles, our farm was an underground railroad hideaway for people escaping from slavery and going toward Chambersburg. Friends there had shown us the methods they used to help others. Our farm became an overnight refuge; it had a hilly southwest corner that helped immensely. We learned to be silent about that. When friends came over to hunt, we'd avoid that corner of the field, not knowing if it was occupied. When we were asked about not hunting there, we would say that it was muddy.

We were pulling weeds in one section when we met someone on horseback. He inquired about a place to eat and rest for the night. My father asked him a searching question, knowing he was hours away from Chambersburg or Hagerstown for what he wanted.

—Are you a person out lookin' for runners or what?

Runners were people labeled slaves escaping from others.

—Sir, I am a photographer from New York City, and I am working out of Washington. My job is to be a reporter for news companies and provide pictures for them. I am not involved in capturing slaves. I ride the countryside here in Pennsylvania and Maryland because this land is progressively changing what with the mule barge canal and now the railroad making the canal seem old fashioned. No sir, I photograph this former western frontier now that it is becoming the launch site to the new west.

—Then by crackie, you'd be welcome to spend the night with our farm family if you wish, said Father, slapping his thigh.

—I'd be most obliged to you, sir, for I have been on my way since sunup. My horse, Smile, could use a break also. Thank you. My name is Alexander Gardner. He extended his hand.

—My name is Harold Darius, and these are my sons, Amos, Daniel, and Bret. We would be pleased to have you as a visitor as we don't have many. You boys work another two hours and come on back to the house for supper. Never you mind chores tonight. Me and Mister, uh, me and our guest will handle that.

It was a night of conversation and fun talk for once. Alexander Gardner did not care to be drawn into Washington talk and the politicians there who knew it all. My sisters, Mary and Gail, being the oldest of us kids, strangely came to supper in Sunday clothes, all fussed up.

—What is it like taking a picture? Amos asked Alexander.

—I really like taking pictures of the mountains here with views down toward the river. It is wonderful to take pictures and show them to others. So many villages and homes now built with people living off the land. This passage through the mountains you live in and to the west is getting very populated.

—One home I found was on a mountainside, looking very neat with the wood all cut and split by the door. It had a small flowerbed with two yellow flowers looking like it had had weeds pulled out a couple of days before. I expected to see the missus just inside the door, as it was open. I hollered a hello and heard nothin'. No sound other than some birds. I looked in, saw no one, and so walked in. I hollered again with no response. I went back outside, but no one showed up even at sundown. I made a meal expecting the home dwellers to return soon, but that open door confused me. I spent the night there and left the next morning, closing the door.

—Was a kitty there when you went in? Oh I hope you took care of it! I wouldn't want something bad to happen to it, Gail said.

—I saw no kitten or any animal, not even in the horse barn, Alexander replied. If I did see one, I'd have not left as I did. And not more than, oh, a week later, I found a small town down by the Potomac River that was burnt to the ground.

The girls being girls thought he was flirting with them when he asked about barn dances and Daisy Mae days where the girls chased boys.

—Wouldn't you like to know, said Mary, the older sister, in a reserved manner.

The next morning came, and we boys stayed in the loft, not wanting to wake anyone. We whispered among ourselves. We heard noise outside and looked out the window. We saw Alexander in the yard, cleaning his camera. We hurried out to look at it.

—Well, good morning, boys. Mighty pleased to see you. Your farm smells sweet this morning.

We didn't say much. We were looking at the first camera we'd ever saw. This contraption on a tripod looked like a square tuft of straw we feed to the horses.

—How can that make a picture when it's all shut up? Amos asked.

As the oldest, hence knowing the most, I piped up.

—Just like when I see something and shut my eyes, my mind keeps it.

—Okay, Merlin. How do you get it out of your mind onto a photograph plate? Amos asked.

I stalled, not knowing.

Alexander removed a picture from his satchel, and we saw our first photograph, a view from a mountaintop looking into a valley.

—Do you know this view? he asked.

We did not. He pointed west of us at the Tuscarora Mountain as we called it.

—I was up there overlooking the valley we are in now and took a picture. I told myself, I sure would like to meet someone down here. Lo and behold, I did last night. Your farm is somewhere over here on this side of the view.

We looked at the picture again and were amazed at the sight. That box could memorize a picture and not forget it.

—You draw so fast and you did that yesterday? You sure are good! Daniel said.

—No, I didn't draw a picture. I took a picture. Later today, after chores, we'll find a bale of hay and I'll take your family picture.

With those words, my life changed.

Later, after he set up the tripod camera and we got dressed, as Momma wanted us looking good, we sat on some bales.

—Now you must sit still for thirty seconds and then I'll show you the magic, Alexander said.

And magic it was. We were sitting still. He slid a wood door open on the box and then shutting it.

—Okay, get up, Alexander said.

Like kids looking at their first foal, what we saw was a smaller box he kept under a black tarp.

—Now I must develop the picture, and then you will see yourself in your first picture.

He poked his head under the black tarp, moved around some, and in a couple of minutes reappeared with a new plate.

—Please don't touch it yet because it's wet. When dry, you can.

We looked at our first family photograph spellbound. We saw the smile on Momma's face and Father's glance at her.

His second-night stay was like a Christmas in July looking at that photograph. The floodgates had opened, and everyone had an object of interest to talk about from ballgames to school.

—You should have seen my snowman last year.

—No, my big pumpkin was better.

—The town parade two years ago—

—No, your—

—Children, please! Momma said. You all have many good things to tell Mr. Gardner, but he can only listen to you one at a time.

She had barely made her plea to us children when Father piped in.

—My bull took the prize last year in plowing the fastest furrow. That would have been a picture, seeing his size.

Alexander sat and smiled listening to the chatter. He had heard it all before from other families about the prettiest baby, whose roof had goats eating grass on it, to farm animals. Funny how a picture, with people having never seen one before, opens the mind to picture taking.

I was sitting quiet most of this time thinking. I looked down, raising my head and opening my mouth to speak, but I couldn't get a word in edgewise until my father made his comment about the bull.

—Is picture taking so easy as you did it? That looks like something I could do, I said.

—When you learn how to take a photograph and then develop it, it's easy. The chemicals and plates are heavy, and I know one job you just might want. If I had you with me to learn photography, we could ride the country, doing pictures as I did today. Then you could do the same kind of pictures anywhere and be paid to do it. A camera is expensive, but you will be known by many people for your picture taking.

I was about to run upstairs and pack, but Momma's look told me whoa. I had seen her look that way when Father screwed up or we kids didn't clean as she wanted, but this look was a kind of a sorry look. Maybe one of knowing it was that time of life when a child had grown and was ready to leave. Looking down and then at Father, she saw an expression on his face and knew he saw what she had seen. Momma came back with a smile and a look of pleasure to me.

—Bret, go if that is what you'd like to do.

I had a talk with Bette and left with Alexander the next day to become a photographer. We traveled by way of Hagerstown to the Potomac River crossing to Harpers Ferry with several nights of camping. Once we reached Harpers Ferry, Alexander and I stayed the night at the home of a person he knew.

Alexander told about the time he had been there before, when John Brown had attacked the federal armory.

—Back in 1859, I was staying in this very room when a loud commotion in town awoke me with guns firing, lots of noise. I thought a bank was being robbed. A robbery in the middle of the night didn't make sense until I awoke more. The fighting was constant for about an hour, and then random shots, and then none. I raised my head and looked out the window, seeing buildings away from me on fire. Then a trio of horses came around the corner, and rifle fire began again. I dove under the bed, being afraid.

—Yelling continued after the shooting stopped, so I went outside to see what was going on. I found out that John Brown was the organizer and he and others had broke into the federal armory to get guns, hoping to arm people enslaved in the South. They were holed up with hostages only to be captured, as you know. I tried to get a photograph, but people near the armory wouldn't hold still for a picture, so I couldn't get one taken. I went on my way to Washington.

His story made me shiver in me, knowing the threats of war were very true with the presidential election soon. After the conviction and hanging in December 1859 of John Brown and his party, anything was possible. That event had been less than a year earlier.

I got a room in Washington and could see the Capitol down the hill from Alexander's office, just around the corner from me. I wrote to

Bette that she should come here so we could be together, but I knew it wouldn't be allowed because of our church teachings. Mail was slow, so it took two weeks getting her letter back, and it was a lonely time for me, my first time away from home. Bette's letter expressed the same desire of wanting to be with me, but we knew it could not happen.

I wandered about Washington and saw so many things I never knew existed. So many buildings, and a sidewalk where only people walked and horses didn't. On the other hand, a fence to keep people away from things. On the farm, we used a fence to keep animals in.

Knowing nothing about the art of photography, I was expected to be Alexander's assistant and do whatever he said for the picture taking. I learned how to arrange people or things, what outfit to wear as a photographer, going for the mail, or mixing chemicals for the photography. And I learned a lot about the camera from setting it up, what a picture wanted to say when taken, and telling the other person to not move.

After six months, I began doing more of the actual work taking pictures. Alexander would patiently show me the details, but he continued the developing of the photograph plates. It felt good working with him, taking photos of the navy fleet sailing into Baltimore and taking President James Buchanan's picture with many special ceremonies at the White House.

Civil War talk became real with the April 1861 attack on Fort Sumter in South Carolina followed by the Baltimore riots on Union forces marching through town. In the midst of Confederate wins, one by one, states joined the Confederate States of America.

Early one morning, Alexander and I had a man-to-man talk. I walked into his office. His solemn frame of mind and stiff lips gave me the sensation my job was on the line.

—Bret, you and I have done quite a lot of photography now, and I like your work. You are learning really well, and I expect you'll want to branch out on your own if you could. You saw how I have to be very visible to people to manage the business. I know people want to get their pictures taken, and we have the equipment with us to do it at a minute's notice. Then to find a person who will pay a good price for other photos we took. Some newspaper editors will pay a penny for a picture when you should get a nickel. You've watched me do that a good deal.

—Yes. That Dermott is always hard on you. I think he sometimes is kidding you and—

—He acts like he's kidding, but he's not, Alexander said, breaking in. That guy would make the buffalo on the nickel look naked if he could sell its hide. We're getting into a civil war, and it could be short or it could be long, but I am planning on traveling to where the fighting is, taking pictures. I don't want to be a target, and I don't want you to be drawn into this. A friend of mine, a photographer from the Indian Wars, was killed. Everywhere will be blood with dead people and animals. I want you to decide if you want to be the courier of my pictures. I have already arranged with Dermott, and he will purchase all photos I— we—turn in. Do you want to stay with me? I must make plans.

I was stunned. My heart was pounding. He had told me something so different from anything I had ever heard or believed. His plan to take photographs of battles and the horrific scenes wouldn't be easy on me, but the idea of being safe and working with others was okay. I waited until I was sure of myself. Before supper, I told him I would work with him.

—I'm pleased to hear that. We shouldn't be in real trouble because we will always be behind the troops. Moreover, we need daylight to take photographs. We'll head to Virginia where the skirmishes are going on. Thank you, Bret.

I wrote to Bette about how I would be involved in these clashes with picture taking. There would be battles that Alexander and I could get photographs of scenes afterward. I wouldn't do any of the fighting. I deeply expressed my love for her and told her that after this war, I was coming home to marry her and live where we had always talked about. I wrote my parents with the news of my getting involved as a photographer. I wrote of how well my father had taught me to protect myself from danger by being careful and Momma teaching me about compassion and care for others.

I also explained to Bette and my parents that a response letter probably wouldn't get to me as I didn't know where I would be. I asked them to pray for me and for all who would be involved in this conflict.

Alexander found out where General Robert E. Lee was, but it took effort and manipulation to arrange a meeting with him.

—I am very honored to be in your presence, General Lee. My name is Alexander Gardner. I hope my assistant, Bret Darius, and I could have a few minutes of your time. We are photographers and wish to use photography to record for history details of your march into Union territory. Then history, a hundred years from now, will see how you defeated the Union by what you did.

—Welcome to our camp. General Lee, sitting at a small desk, broke into a big Southern smile. He stood and offered his hand to Alexander and me. His grip was strong.

—Alexander and Bret, this will make us very happy and more resolute in our desire to get across the Potomac River and show them a few more of our intentions.

He looked out the tent flap and hollered.

—Sergeant, please get these gentlemen a good set of Southern clothes. They are going to be with us.

—We will remain behind any battle line and try to be not easily seen by Union troops, so our photography will not interfere with any of your plans, Alexander said.

—Well, thank you. This will be a first time for photography to record us getting the Yanks. I am planning an attack on Bull Run, and I am seriously considering after Bull Run to cross the Potomac near Harpers Ferry. John Brown did show the way there. Come, have a hearty meal of smoked deer with us, and tell me more about this plate photography. You say this can … The general talked on as we walked toward the officers' mess tent.

We followed his army to the first battle at Bull Run in Virginia. There, I shared an early morning breakfast with Woody from North Carolina and Mike from Alabama. Both expected a conflict that day. Woody fiddled with the coffee getting it just right as he said.

—The Union boys are used to living in big cities, and they don't know what a gun looks like till they're hunting.

—Yep, Mike said. My brother up in Philly said his friend told him he has to look for the owner's manual to figure out how to load it. Then I wrote him a letter to pass on to that fellow. Tell him bullets need to be loaded only after they spent the night in a bucket of oil. They will fly faster!

I broke into a big laugh with them as we were thinking about that battlefield with half the Union troops sitting down, reading their owners' manuals.

—I bet my mare carries more guns than the Yankees do! Woody boasted.

I held my side with the laughter breaking my funny bone.

That evening after the battle, it was a ghastly surreal for me not seeing the men I had talked with that morning. Many of both sides were lying dead from guns and shrapnel.

We followed the CSA Army to the second victory at Bull Run in Virginia with photographs of the various back-and-forth battle movements. Then we followed a brigade of Virginians under Colonel Thomas J. "Stonewall" Jackson, who stood their ground. A counterattack by Confederates sent the Union troops withdrawing, and it turned into a rout as they discarded their arms and equipment. Influential persons, including congressmen and their families, were having picnics and watching as the battle went on. When it turned, they attempted to flee in their carriages and blocked roads back to Washington. We made a humorous photograph of that. Another of our incredible photographs was a new sight in the battle sky of a balloon used for aerial scouting by the Union. It was floating like a giant lily pad on a pond.

Again, after the battle, I faced the reality that the men I had seen or talked with before were dead. This conflict was not a gentlemen's dispute but a to-the-death war. Bull Run was the moment both sides realized it wouldn't be easy.

Preparing for the planned attack on the Northern states, Brigadier General John Bell Hood commanded a division of the First Corps and wanted his inspired words to give good spirits to General Lee's planned march across the Potomac after their night bivouac on the Virginia riverbank. A rest period with good drink and food would nourish their bodies.

—We have the North here in our sights, and I see no campfires in Maryland, General Lee said. They are scared of us, knowing we're at the door. We will win this skirmish and take Philadelphia before it snows. Then we will ring the bell of liberty for the Confederate States of America and proclaim freedom and liberty for our beliefs. They do not know what they say. If it came to a conflict of arms, the war will last at least four years. The Northern politicians will not appreciate the determination and pluck of the South, and Southern politicians do not appreciate the numbers, resources, and patient perseverance of the North.

Just over the river into Maryland is the town of Sharpsburg, nestled in a valley with farm fields of corn and grass. Its beauty presented a sense of peace and serenity. This was the place the Union forces knew General Lee was setting up to pass through on his way north as a mislaid Secret Order 191 by General Lee was obtained by Union Major General McClellan, and the general made a decision to stop the attacks there.

Scouts were observing each other, and the sides were placing themselves for skirmishes. Charges by one side or the other occurred through the vast plain, and generals constantly shifted troops to pull back or advance as they deemed necessary. A cavalcade of horses and artillery would appear on a hillside or in a street battle. The cacophony of artillery and gunfire around the homes in Sharpsburg kept residents inside or running to caves along the new C&O Canal. Barely was an advance made than an abrupt end sweep of troops would cause the battle line to reverse.

Alexander and I were ensconced behind the Dunker Church, which showed damage from artillery fragments. The soldiers were moving around so much that it was hard to see the battle lines. The continuous sound of rifles, artillery, shouting, and screaming made any talk between Alexander and me nearly impossible. Horsemen would suddenly appear behind us, and I wished I had a shovel to dig a deep hole and crawl into it.

Alex suddenly stood up and hustled to a side of the church away from the oncoming horsemen. I followed, and we got safely out of sight of them. Then I saw a cut on his forehead and felt fear of being hurt myself as he wiped at it. It continued to weep. Our backs were to the wall. A view of the battle lay in front of us. A cannon would fire, and we would see the effect of the shell blasting a furrow in the soil with troops collapsing. It appeared the shell had struck both Confederate and Union troops, and it vividly described the saying that war was hell.

Alexander touched my shoulder and signaled to follow him toward the woods as the fighting was getting closer to us again. I assumed we were leaving as the photograph equipment we hid was there. With our backs to the carnage, we managed to reach the trees. Collapsing, he lay against a tree and continued wiping his wound. I tried not to look alarmed, but he saw it in me and assured me we would be safe.

The roars of battle became softer and then louder as battles maneuvered around us. It was not until after sundown that the firing slowed. Alexander stood up and in a soft voice said he was going into Sharpsburg and would return with horses so we could ride away before dawn.

—Keep low and quiet. I'll be back, he said.

Calming down from the terror of the day, I became hungry and knew what we had carried was gone. There was nowhere safe to go. It would be a long night. A noise from behind became louder. I thought Alexander was returning sooner than I thought he would. It got louder as if it were him, but it stopped. No sounds. Not even a cricket. It stayed that way for some time. I threw a branch well away from me. It hit the field with a soft thud, but no other sound. My mind filled with terror again, not knowing what to expect or how to react. I thought about Bette. How I wished I were with her.

Sleep had welcomed me, but the sound of horses awoke me in the predawn. I looked around. I saw gray objects moving against the darkness. No Alexander. I prayed he was near. I could hear wagon wheels turning near the church, but I could see nothing. A group of soldiers began to step march. The sounds of their boots faded. The sky lightened, and I saw the absolute carnage. Bodies everywhere lying atop one another. The sound from last night must have been an injured soldier walking and then falling.

It appeared troops were gathering to go somewhere, but when I saw artillery lining up to the southeast, I was again in a possible battle zone of artillery. I needed a more secure spot well away, and it needed to be done soon as the sun was about to break.

I slipped deeper among the trees and ran into one that had fallen some time ago. I lay beside it for protection. Artillery fire began. Debris and tree limbs crashed down. I wrapped my arms around my head and ears to try to quiet the noise. The shells fell in a scattered pattern and shook the ground, causing me to shiver in fear of death. There was no safety for my soul other than in my mind. I prayed to God for safety. Why oh why had I wanted to be involved in this?

A blinding flash of light burst in my mind. I went into a motionless state. When I regained consciousness, it felt like the weight of the world was on my body. Struggling to get free only caused my arm to throb in pain. I passed out.

The pain in my arm awakened me, and I realized movement was not possible. The throbbing in my arm caused me to cry out in pain and terror, not knowing if the sound would cause me to be shot again. The excruciating pain caused me to think anything was better than that. I lost consciousness again.

I heard nothing, not even an insect chirp. I could smell nothing and felt no pain. I began to think I had died and was in a passage to heaven or hell. I thought of leaving my family and all my desires to do the things Bette and I had dreamed about. Was it gone forever? What was happening to me?

Coughing blood, I began to think I was buried but still alive. I could wiggle my toes, but my fingers felt immobile. The pain returned, and my wet body throbbed as I vainly tried to move. Spitting blood or something out of my mouth, I hollered, but my swollen tongue couldn't complete a word. I passed into unconsciousness again.

Not knowing where I was, whether it was day or night, I felt the heaviness on my body had shifted. I heard the thump of objects being moved. A burden was lifted off my body, pulling me onto my back. A blurred vision was all I saw.

—Here's a live one! someone yelled.

Passing in and out of reality, I was still lying where I had hid myself or so I thought. I managed to sit up after several tries, and my blurred vision saw a cloudy sky. I painfully tried to touch my face and discovered my hand and half my arm were gone. How was I still living? Why had I not bled to death? Me, injured and feeling the agony of a loss.

Stunned by the discovery, I slumped back and believed my life was over. Shock from the injury and the weakness in my body made me think as best I could. I had somehow not been killed. My arm was gone, but I hadn't bled to death. There had to be a reason in life for me. Someone had covered the shattered stump with a bloody binding. I kept asking myself, *Why, why, why?*

I spotted the church and resolved to drag myself toward the smell of wood smoke. I trusted help was there, but I couldn't move. It wasn't until someone gently touched my shoulder that I became conscious.

—You're hurt, and I'll get you assistance.

—I have a Confederate uniform on. I live in Pennsylvania. I—

—Don't matter who you are, interrupted the lady. You are a person needing help, and I will give you aid.

—Thank you. I'm so thirsty and hungry, please, I mumbled.

—I'll be back with water and someone for you.

Assistance was not available until well into the night. A horse wagon took me into Sharpsburg to a home on Mechanics Street. There, a retired doctor from Boonsboro came the next day with his doctor's bag and sewed up my shattered limb as best he could. He stated that surgery would be necessary to effect a better-looking limb and that if it healed with minimal infection, it would be okay.

I later learned the owner of the home was the Wingents. They treated me like a family member. I wanted to help them but could do little.

I wondered what Bette would think about me being this way. My letter to her expressed the great remorse I was feeling. I also mailed a letter to my parents. I was sobbing with thoughts about what my parents would think of me. I sat on the porch for days in Sharpsburg reflecting on what had happened and what my life would be like. I dreaded to read my parents' response. A letter from them stated their relief to know I was alive and gave the date they would arrive to take me home. That increased my anxiety.

My parents rode a horse wagon south through Hagerstown to Sharpsburg on the Hagerstown Pike. At first, I could not look at them for the shame I felt for letting them down. My momma was crying. Later, she told me they were tears of joy because I was living.

—You did what you thought was right. God kept you alive for us and for you. You have a duty in this life yet to achieve, my father said, which made me feel better.

They stayed overnight with the Wingents, and we left for home the next day.

It took many rough months for me to recuperate. I had countless days of regretful thinking about what I had done and been involved in. At times, my missing fingers felt as if they itched, but I could do nothing about it. I wondered about Alexander Gardner. I wrote to his Washington, DC office and heard he was still alive, taking photographs.

I found out only after I was home trying to mend that my brothers had joined the 126th Pennsylvania Infantry in 1862, with training at Camp Biddle in Greencastle and a later transfer to Washington, DC. After the war, Daniel returned safe, but Amos had been wounded near Petersburg, Virginia, and after a short time in a hospital had died.

A friend told me about his daughter, Dolly Harris, who was seventeen at the time General George Pickett and his men marched through Greencastle toward Gettysburg in 1863.

—Pickett's troops were moving through town on Carlisle Street, and she ran into the street in front of the leader of them, waving the stars and stripes in his face and hollering they were traitors to their country, cutthroats, and plunderers. Ol' Pickett stood up in his stirrups, removed his hat, and saluted Dolly. I guess he thought she was waving that flag as a courageous young lady. And dang if Pickett's men also saluted her and the division's band serenaded her with "Dixie."

I laughed at that. It was my first laugh in a long time.

After the Battle of Gettysburg, I saw General Lee's army one last time as he retreated to Virginia. A cavalry unit escorted a large wagon train nearly eighteen miles long that was carrying Confederate wounded as it passed through Greencastle. I heard a few men had attacked the wagons with axes and hatchets and were able to disable several of the wounded before they were chased away by the Confederate cavalry.

Those months at home recovering gave me many hours to reflect about the tragedy of war. Not just to me but for many Union and Confederate soldiers who were involved for reasons not really understood by us. It did set a profound change in lifestyles, and many had been killed or wounded for it. I resolved to work with other injured as best I could. I wanted to assist them in their healing. I drove a horse carriage reconstructed as an ambulance. For me, it was an occasion to lend a hand to others getting to hospitals for treatment. I wanted to never forget the battles and the deaths of soldiers and families because of people's attitude toward others.

Bette and I married on October 9, 1863, at the Antrim Mennonite Church in Greencastle, which remained a big part of our lives. We lived on Old Howards Mill Road, and two girls became part of our family. After high school, Bernadette stayed active in a local business, and Ida was later a professor at Penn State. They were both empathetic and helpful with others.

I became more active in our community, attending borough meetings and doing volunteer work with organizations in town and the area. I ran for office and was elected to the borough council.

I continued with photography. The pictures I took of families hang in many living rooms. Photos of views overlooking the magnificent valleys and the meandering Potomac River made me appreciate what I saw. Bette became a photographer with me, and she saw more scenes of beauty than I did. Her pictures of a field of children playing or a farm in the process of harvesting meant that nature was managing the process of life. Humanity tries to change the nature of things to its advantage, but in the end, nature makes the necessary correction to humanity.

Bette and I used our senior years as a time of enjoying each other, traveling the countryside, and riding fancy trains to visit friends. We visited the steel mills in Pittsburgh, marveled at the smoke-filled valley, and saw American steel moving by rail in all directions. We traveled as far west as the Ohio River, feeling it was far enough away from home for us.

We returned to Sharpsburg, Maryland, in September 1867 for the town's memorial service to remember all the soldiers and people who lived near the battlefield who had been killed or wounded. We also made pleasant visits to the Wingents not to keep in mind those traumatic moments but to enjoy each other as close friends. They received our Pennsylvanian good food and hospitality on their visits to our home.

Occasionally, Bette and I return to the Antietam battlefield and walked in that former field of intentions. As I look over this valley and at the Dunker Church, an echo of the Civil War, of this field as it was once before, is in my mind. Full of screams, rifle and artillery fire, but now the quiet, somber silence of hearing all the fallen soldiers and their crying on the field.

Nosy Billy

—Billy, quit digging in your nose or your finger will get caught in there. Please, that's so messy, my mother told me.

Probably a million times since I don't know when, she'd advise me and I would withhold my nose mining till we were not in sight of one another. If blowing my nose didn't do the job, I tried a shovel.

Funny, I saw her doing it herself several times. Maybe as a person gets older, fingers get smaller or the memory forgets what a person is supposed to do or not do.

One Tuesday evening in my room, a nose itch started, and I began a snotball exploration, catching it on the first attempt and proceeding with the extraction. Halfway out, my finger stopped moving, and I pulled a little more with no movement. I figured that booger was bigger than when it had materialized. I tried moving my finger back and forth with no success. It was as if the nostril had collapsed. I began to get a little uptight, particularly about Mom seeing me this predicament.

My finger must have suddenly swelled. I tried to relax, so I sat for a few minutes trying to calm down. Any effort to remove the finger made it feel like superglue had been involved. I yanked, and it jerked my head forward. Closing my mouth, I blew my nose; the other nostril blew like a steam whistle. Squeezing it shut with the free hand, I blew again. My cheeks ballooned from the pressure with no change at the finger-plugged nostril cave-in.

I gave up and decided there was no choice but to go to Mom. I went toward the living room but turned just before entry and walked toward her backward. I slowly turned. She saw me. Her mouth dropped open and her eyes popped open.

I mumbled about the problem. She decided, just as a mother would, to solve the stalemate I was in.

—Let me look at this. You know I warned you.

A shimmer appeared in her eyes. Was it from a medical emergency, or did she see that booger was really a living thing?

—I'll get a warm washrag and place it on your nose.

But leaving the cloth there resulted in no change.

—Let's try an ice cube to shrink it, she suggested, but that produced no result either.

—Well, to the emergency room we'll go.

She had been right. A creature like a miniature slug in my nose had grabbed my finger. She comforted me. She wrapped her arm around me as we walked to the car. I heard a slight snicker from her as she started the car and backed up. She abruptly stopped halfway to the road. She gripped the steering wheel and appeared to be holding her breath as if her diagnosis of my situation had turned for the worst. She looked down toward her feet and exhaled with a strange look on her face. I couldn't tell what was going on, but when she again looked at me, her sardonic expressing surprised me.

—I know what will work for you. It just occurred to me.

—What?

—Straighten your finger. Try that.

Duh.

UFOs Are Martians on Earth

In a package mailed in 2023 to many national libraries around the world was a revelation that changed the archeological history of Earth. The human race may have evolved with humanity still living with monkeys without certain help. The package contained a digital disc with audio and video content revealing a startling history of Martian life on Earth. It was considered a hoax until the video on the disc solved historical mysteries and revelations by the US government of their knowledge about Martians on Earth came out. Upon that disclosure, talk shows and hastily published books were devoured by a public eager to know more.

The following can be described only by the message on the disc.

Announcement

We are using words and terms currently used on Earth so you can understand what is presented on this disc.

This is translated into many of the languages on Earth in descriptive terms. It concerns the inhabitants of the fourth planet from the Sun, called Mars, in their moving to Earth. Mental telepathy is the planet language of Mars. We are peace loving and are not conquerors, as various inhabitants in other dimensions are. We lived here as an unknown, unseen society and assisted with idea building but did no work for you.

We are passing this information on to you because you are not alone and may visit other planets or dimensions sooner than you think. They may be more or less advanced than you. Likewise, other universe civilizations visiting Earth might see the conditions and either move on or take over the Earth. Earthlings might be trained by other societies for their purposes or be used as subjects for lab experiments.

With your travel to other solar masses now beginning, the enormous technical advances you have made and world events caused by Earthlings, Martian colonies on Earth have determined a return to Mars is in our best interest. Remember that we are a peace-loving society.

Devoid of artifacts, we never knew the origin of the Martian race. History is not important to us when our culture has lived for millions of years. Perhaps we are immigrants from another dimension living as an underground society since asteroids and radiation from the Sun produce problems for us. We rely on water and vegetarian food in pill form for nutrients. Our birth process is by egg, a more civilized process of procreation.

When it was inhabited, Mars was a one-world government named Xerbis. Mature Martians have an excellent memory, and our hatched young at the age of about one Mars orbit around the Sun attain the ability to talk telepathically. After four Mars orbits of the Sun, education was no longer needed, as the young had the knowledge to use.

The colonies, being underground, faced various problems and were permitted to govern as they needed. Having time travel as the vehicle of conveyance, we traveled to various galaxies and dimensions sightseeing, but many Martians tended to stay in their colony. Why leave when you see the same thing everywhere? With freedom of movement, you can visit anywhere, any time.

Eons ago, before Earth coalesced into a planet, Martian scientists realized our planet was cooling and losing its atmosphere. What to do was debated for five hundred Mars orbits, one thousand of your years. Politicians of the ruling colony established homes deeper into Mars but could not find a viable source of oxygen. Mars scientists repeatedly told them that oxygen was being lost and the limited amount of underground water on Mars was not feasible to convert to oxygen for breathing as it was needed for nutrients and drinking. The politicians established a study group to conduct research. That took fifty Martian orbits to verify. When oxygen in colonies 500 meters underground began to approach 9 percent, concerned colonists issued a warning; a planetary search needed finalization and moving toward an exit sphere must be done. Our politicians, being logical, put it to a debate that lasted another thousand Mars orbits.

Martian explorers teleported to many planets in various dimensions, searching for a new home planet. Reports detailed conditions varying from no atmosphere to gaseous or liquid masses. In a particular visit to Xuna in the fifth dimension, we discovered a mass with oxygen but inhabitants who continually fought. We considered this as an unsuitable settlement for our docile lifestyle. On an excursion to Venus, we found it to be too hot with little land mass and no oxygen in the atmosphere.

A telepathically communicated message from an exploratory ship gives you a view of Earth from our point of view. Earth was determined suitable except for its weather conditions caused by the tilt of the planet's axis, but a planetary nudge would correct that.

After many visits, the third planet from the Sun was determined the best. Earth has about 20 percent oxygen in the atmosphere, whereas we live with 12 percent.

We did move to Earth. We settled high on mountains to limit the oxygen intoxication of Martians by the oxygen-rich atmosphere. We built guidance markers in South America for our followers to the site we decided on. These landmarks are visible only from space and are used to guide colonies to the mountain we selected.

The amount of water on this planet is staggering to us. Clouds generated from water evaporation are a natural system we had never seen. The fierce weather storms here involve water, not sand, and represent a new geography with winds controlling the water.

We have established Martian faces on an island in the southern portion of the Pacific Ocean facing the sunrise. Also on the mountain but facing away from the sunrise are immense runways for vessel landings. Because of gravity, teleportation did not work here, so smaller vessels were the only method to navigate on our arrival. An icon of Mars is near the landing site.

Having explored Earth, our purpose was to find better sites for us. The excessive oxygen here is a real problem. We had to wear masks at lower mountain levels to keep our oxygen intake controlled so we could grow a hydroponic garden. We are vegetarians.

We searched the surface and found several mountains that were candidates of interest, but we rejected them because of extreme cold for garden seed growth. The search continued with no real results.

—Why don't we build it under the water? a little girl asked her mother. Upon hearing that, we were stunned.

Maybe the too-rich oxygen atmosphere of Earth had made us drunk, but a child had it right with her question. It could easily control oxygen levels, provide the lifestyle we preferred, and give us the feeling of being at home on Earth. The child's name was Xinon, so the first colony under seawater was named Xinonville in her honor.

Earth is very diverse in material, and we constructed the first underwater colony during one Earth orbit and enjoyed it. Our undersea colony used kelp for vegetarian food and saltwater converted to drinking water and fuel. With colonies here, we had a method to live as long as we wanted and planned to do so.

Reports on Mars spread about the first colony's success, and all Martians immigrated to undersea colonies. We left the home planet with a face monument of our existence there. Senior-citizen Martians forced to move to Earth hated the idea of living in a remote unit not on native soil. Slowly, as all Homo sapiens did, we acclimatized to the stronger gravity of Earth.

Xinonville was the ruling colony and directed that there would be no contact with Earthlings other than for scientific purposes. Martians could go to the surface to view Earthlings covertly. We first used a dinosaur mock-up as our vessel when we arrived, as they were prevalent. It became what Earthlings called the Loch Ness monster.

Later, you called a Martian vessel capable of teleporting a UFO. Eons ago, a rogue planet beyond Mars was struck by an asteroid and shattered. One piece struck Earth and ended the dinosaur era, as Earth-bound people called the giants then living.

Why do we cruise in a space vehicle? Some of us love to sightsee and hover or travel at 400 kilometers per hour, using hyperactive speed for time travel. It is a pleasure to see Mars again, the rings of Saturn, and the triple-sun cluster in the eighth dimension. We saw on Earth how well our guidelines for the pyramids had been followed, and we saw the manned landing on the moon later. The sights on Earth we can see from space are wonderful—from the northern lights to hurricanes. Titans from Jupiter call hurricanes a mass circulator.

Rogue pilots would take a ship and fly off to cruise the universe because they could. Their style was flying and looking with other craft following, getting into a formation shape and cruise as bikers do.

A new method of communication here between colonies involved low-frequency video and text messages. Using the Darzu language, the shrieks sounded as whales or porpoises to Earthian aquatic scientists.

Should we communicate with Earthlings? Why?

You lost the ability to telepathically communicate when your humanoid ancestors discovered fire and started speaking in many languages. Earth must learn telepathy, which is used by all other cultures. There are no words in mind talk, just ideas that are shared.

We did not disclose to you solutions to future problems but have guided you to use the "aha" factor for insight into possible solutions. Insight leads to inspiration from another well-used phrase, "What if ...?"

Martian colonies previously viewed people on Earth as a life form in development. The knowledge level after Homo sapiens evolved from monkeys was at the kindergarten level till we nudged you into walking in the upright position, which led you to think. The human race, as you call yourself, determined gestation must be called pregnancy. Your political correctness began in 5627 BC. Early Earthians drank water like animals and used rocks to cut up meat.

We decided to have no contact after that first nudge but just watch to observe your learning ability. It took

4,000 year before the first million Earthlings were living.

Our underwater colonies are not discernible by any means due to our cloaking technology. Your submarines are capable of diving to 1,000 feet, and your sonar can go 10,000 feet deeper, but that is not close to the depth we live.

People on Earth matured very fast. Your technology and curiosity led you to send spacecraft to other spheres, including Mars, to learn about our planet. A face monument on Mars was identified by your first satellite to Mars in 1997 and is at 26.5 degrees north latitude. You call it a curious sand mound, but it is the Martian face we left behind.

Earthlings theorized that Mars was in the process of forming, that life had not evolved. It was also hypothesized Martians may have moved to another planet or were dead. However, we knew how to disguise former colony surface activity from Earth science.

Wars on Mars were sporadic; one colony would want the site another colony had and fight for it. We view wars on Earth as colony fighting. We didn't expect you to develop nuclear weapons so soon after you learned to fly. We could not discern a civilization in any dimension that had provided that information to you. Atomic weapons made us anxious because civilizations in other dimensions know these well. Your Zinger has us very worried.

After the atomic fission bombs were used in one Earthian orbit, it was decided that further surveillance must be conducted in 1947 as to the intent of a country called America. Newscasts around the world reported UFO sightings, while others called it interesting or said nothing. An American newscast reported a UFO crash, but the government said it had been a balloon that crashed.

To decrease threats of conflict on Earth, we decided to use anti-noise technology to cancel or garble threatening messages between countries making it appear that an equipment malfunction had occurred.

Your satellite photography in the sixties was good but grainy. We saw a problem of spy-versus-spy reading each other's photos and decided to enter a communication correction so the photography could be viewed as scenes of distortion. Only until you developed digital photography did our analog pulse correction no longer work.

Xinonville dictated that our robots were to appear like Earthlings and intermingle with you for observation. Our robots spoke various languages fluently and "dated" and "married" other robots to continue the illusion. Robotic cameras transmitted what they saw to our colonies, and it was revealing.

Earth as you call it is not alone. There are many colonies from other dimensions using clones of themselves also mingling with you. Using dimensional knowledge, teleportation is practical to everywhere.

We decided to return to our home planet, and the homecoming announcement was met with great delight. Our colonies on Earth had matured; we decided Earth had come of age. Our program of seeing the formation of your civilization had succeeded with astounding results. Because we did not alter your brain or body chemistry, you used knowledge you had; it just needed the kick-start we gave. Your creativity will allow you to unlock the secrets of the dimensions. Concerning dimensions, think quantum.

We also decided to leave behind small robotic devices as observers. They have a small problem we want to make you aware of. They were designed to look like the brown mamorated bug you call the stinkbug. One of our junior scientists had inadvertently programmed a bug into the bug. Two devices were unexpectedly released among the bugs on Earth while they were meant to mingle with neighborhood insects and look like cicadas. We designed its fuel supply to smell like the stinkbug when squished.

Thus my friends, we have reached a point of departure with the end of this recording.

There followed a sound of a needle making the proverbial scratching sound at the end of an LP.

Crackers

—Waiter! There's a fly in my soup!

—Is he swimming or just floating?

—Just close your eyes and eat the soup.

—Put some crackers in your soup. The fly will disappear.

—Can I introduce to you the cockroach muffin? Or how about our mouse meatloaf? Or a lice salad? Excuse me, nice salad?

—I don't see a fly. Maybe you already ate it.

—The fly can go where it wants. We don't have a no-trespassing rule here.

—There is not a no-fly rule in this restaurant.

—Please sir, not so loud or everyone will want one.

—You're a frequent customer here, so we give a fly on every ten visits. Less-frequent visitors are given a fly every five visits.

—Why are you complaining? You need more protein.

—Oh, the fly. It's certified disease-free. The manager will give you a copy of the certificate.

—It's only one fly. What's the problem here? Just eat around it.

—One fly and you think it's a problem? Have you been to that clip joint on 8th Street? They deliver four per plate. And you complain about one here?

—I'm opposed to animal torture. Please don't kill it.

—What am I supposed to do, call 911?

—Well, what you won't eat the fly will.

—Don't worry about it. You'll eat more of the soup than the fly will.

—Sir, you asked for chef's choice on the soup. What's the problem here?

—Okay. Would you prefer the American, Asian, or French fly?

—If I may say, my preference for fly soup is to add a frog. The frog gets the fly and you get the soup.

—Shall I get the flycatcher?

—Did the fly attack or present you with a physical hazard? Otherwise, I can't do anything. A fly is a fly.

—May I say, sir, the fly is a distraction to our customers' valued opinions. But one fly ranks next to having a rare steak when you requested it be well done. It often happens but only from order misreading in the kitchen by the chef. Maybe my spelling confused their logic. Or their two-second reading of an order. C'est la vie.

—What's the problem with just one fly?

—Would you like some fly seasoning?

—We hear this often from customers. My suggestion to them is to eat around the fly.

—Can I help you? Well, what do you need?

—Will this be one ticket or two on this meal?

—Well, do you want a fly or a mosquito? In my opinion, a fly is better because a mosquito is a bloodsucking vampire.

—The soup came from the kitchen clean. Did you invite a guest to your meal? We don't like customers doing that.

—The fly is our secret waiter. He's seeing if you'll want something else.

—Would you like some fly spray, Raid, or red pepper?

American Dating Blunders

Wrong Moves

When I go on a date to dinner or a movie, I try to meet my date's expectations and desires. Because I'm male, my expectations of her often don't match her desires, so I have to be flexible. This means I may not be eating spaghetti or watching Tom Cruise.

She suggested having braised beef on oranges and later we'd watch an old movie, *Born Free*. Having never ate the one or seen the other, I said yes.

The braised beef was good. Should have tried it years ago. *Born Free* was okay, but I yawned fifteen minutes into it. She asked me how I liked it. I said it was interesting, but that brought on her complaint that I didn't appreciate how wildlife had an important effect on nature. I didn't respond. That was a bad choice. Now I'm accused of ignoring her. I guess this date had a real "The End" to it.

Dating a Nerd and Finding Her

Most TV shows portray nerds as wearing large glasses and sporting pocket packs loaded with colored pens and a calculator. When I met this woman, she had none of the equipment. After an hour of conversation, it was obvious she was a bona-fide nerd. Every subject we discussed, she'd take the lead and know it all. I'd get a complete history of its origin, learn where it's going, and all the history in between. I was damned if I didn't get the history of verbs from their Greek or French roots to how they evolved into modern-day English. She obviously studied word genealogy and dictionaries.

I decided it was time to take her home. At the door, we hugged. I asked for a kiss.

—Would you like a cheek kiss, lip kiss, French kiss, or …?

God!

Dating a Neurotic Organic Woman

I met Cherie, a homebody, through a friend who said Cherie was introverted. I asked questions about Cherie, but my lady friend took me to her house for coffee. We greeted each other and sat at a table. The talk was general-interest subjects. Cherie's main interest was in looking down. She would talk only if she was asked question.

—What was your name again? was her only question. She wasn't engaging in the discussion.

Not getting any information about her or how she lived made me curious. Maybe it was because her girlfriend was there. So I asked her out, and after a pause, she said sure. I suggested we go to Pizza Hut the following Friday night.

—Well, I guess that place would be okay with me. Cherie exhaled slowly and looked down.

I had a feeling that she would rather not but agreed just to get us out of her house.

Disaster.

I walked Cherie to my car several days later and was going to open the door for her.

—No, I'll get it.

At the restaurant, she drank only water and wanted no pizza because of the cheese and meat, she said.

—Cherie, why did you say this place was okay when you won't have anything to eat? Are you feeling all right? I hoped we'd have a pleasant evening, but now I'm confused.

—I'm a vegetarian. Cheese comes from cows' milk. It's terrible how they force cows to give up their milk.

She ate breadsticks. I was tempted to ask her what a cow did if its udder was full. Stop eating? But I wisely kept my mouth shut.

If I asked her any other question or comment, she'd answer most of the time with a yes, no, or I don't know. She asked me nothing. We were there for thirty minutes. That was fifteen minutes too long.

—I'll walk myself to the door. That was her fourth complete sentence of the date delivered when we reached her home.

—Okay, bye, I replied.

I got home and headed to the mirror to see if a large capital L was on my forehead.

Dating a Sergeant

I knew one girl from high school nicknamed Plain Jane. She joined the army when we graduated. She was in town on a thirty-day leave. When I found out about it, I asked her to our high school football game homecoming.

I wore my baseball cap backward, my football jersey, and a pair of well-worn jeans—the style of dress seven years earlier. I smiled. I planned to have a great night. I noticed her doorknob was either new or spit-shined to perfection. She opened the door. I was surprised to see her wearing her army inspection uniform. She inspected me top to bottom.

—Dale, I see we have a problem here. I cannot be seen with a person who looks homeless. We'll go to your place for better clothes.

My smile turned to shock. She was a sergeant. Her military training had turned her into Ms. Perfection.

I was tempted to have her go to my closet and pick what I was expected to wear, but I didn't. She probably would have dressed me in my suit with clean underwear. I had worn the pair I had on for over an hour by then.

We went to the game and met many old classmates. She would yell during the game as if she were on a battlefield. I think everyone there heard her. Several times when she gave a long banshee yell, the people in front of us had to cover their ears.

At halftime, our team was ahead, and we went to the lunch wagon for some snacks.

—I'll have two hotdogs with relish, onion, mustard, and ketchup. And a Pepsi. What can I get you? I asked her.

—No you do not, she said. She turned to the woman taking orders.

—We'll have two hotdogs with one squirt of ketchup each and two coffees.

She turned to me.

—One for you and the other for me. Onions ruin your breath.

So I was considered careless in my dressing and eating habits. I was on the verge of starvation. She paid with what looked like dollars printed yesterday. Very crisp, no corner folds, no marks.

I began to feel like her K-9 dog, so I lagged behind as she carried the meal at chest level to the bleachers. I didn't eat until she unwrapped her hotdog and applied the army technique to take a bite. I watched and tried to copy her, but Plain Jane scowled when I opened the wrapper upside down. I slurped the hot coffee. Another scowl. She sipped.

The second half began. Her bellowing got louder when we fell behind and lost. I sensed she wanted to vault the fence, get into the coach's face, and make him do twenty pushups and four laps around the track.

I had planned to go to the nightclub, dance a little, and listen to the band. I hoped she would loosen up, so I suggested we do that.

—No, it's 2230 hours, and I get up at 0500 hours for my exercise regimen.

I took her home in a kind of shock. What book was she following? She had been fun in high school, and I know she had had sexual affairs back then, but she was carrying herself so pristine and proper.

Being a Veggie and Trying to Love a Buffet Lady

I decided to be a vegan and live that lifestyle for six months to check it out. Maybe the meat I digested was altering my thinking. I found the cooking was a lot easier and less greasy. This was going to be cool!

I shopped the organic stores, read about what was good for me, and began exercising and walking more.

At the gym, I met a woman who exercised regularly, was slim, smiled a lot, and was very friendly. We talked several times a week and became friends. I asked her out for dinner on a night I knew she didn't exercise. She said she liked buffets because you could choose what you wanted and how much of it. I agreed because they always have big salad bars, which was perfect for me.

At the buffet, she started with a good salad, went back for a plate of chicken, went back for fish, went back for meatloaf, went back for a baked potato and a big dollop of sour cream. Then a plate of fruit. My God! Is this why she exercises so much? She ate more during that meal than I ate all week! She was a buffetaholic.

—I don't eat this much every day. Maybe once a week when I come here, she told me.

Yeah, right. The manager must groan when he sees her in line.

We went back to her house, and she invited me in.

—Would you like a coffee?

—Sure, I replied.

—Enjoy, she said as she brought a big plate of cookies to the living room.

At the buffet, I'd had a large salad and was still stuffed. To be gracious, I had one cookie while she had one after another. She must have an afterburner for a digestion system to handle that entire intake.

After half an hour, I left. We hugged at the door.

—See you at the gym tomorrow? she asked.

Whew!

Late-Night Show

We set up a date after she had completed her shift at the bistro where we had met. Those working there knew I was waiting for her to finish. I sat at a booth. A 6:00 a.m. breakfast was our plan.

I had come in sleepy and dragging at five that morning and tried to get fully awake so we could get a good exchange of feelings started.

Andrea came into the dining area from the rear with three plates on her arms and two cups in her hands. I'd seen that balancing act so many times. I was glad they have that skill. We smiled at each other as she went by.

—Hey, that trapeze act with those plates was something else, I said as she walked back.

—Yeah, I sometimes think it will fall, but I can't do anything about it or everything else would go. I've been lucky all these years. I better get moving. I have another armload for the other side. See you in a while, she said as she smiled a good one at me.

My emotions took a leap knowing she was thinking of me. I expected we'd have an interesting date that morning. I knew from working a second or graveyard shift myself that people need time to unwind afterward.

I didn't see her after that early morning chat, so figured she was working in the kitchen. The clock showed 6:00 a.m., then 6:10. By 6:20, I was wondering about her. She couldn't have forgotten. We'd talked less than half an hour earlier!

I asked a waitress about Andrea.

—She left because she had a date today, she said.

I laughed because I knew how tough the night shift could be.

—Are you her date? She looked quizzically at me.

—Well, yeah. We were talking just half an hour ago.

What was I to do? I put my head between my hands. I considered my options. I knew her name and where she worked, but not her phone number, where she lived, or even her last name.

—Ma'am, I asked you about Andrea just a bit ago. Do you know her phone number?

—I'm sorry, I don't.

—Would the manager know? I was getting desperate.

—Oh yes, but he won't get here until, oh, about eight.

I mentally moaned. She'd probably gone home or somewhere. I was about to blow a gasket. Should I wait or go? Should I return tonight and hope she was working? Should I put my tail between my legs and stay home? I picked option two.

—Ma'am, I hate to keep pestering you, but can you tell me if Andrea works tonight please?

She went into the office. She returned.

—Yes, tonight at ten.

—Thank you.

The day was different from the start. It was like watching a timepiece. It would double its Murphy's Law ability to slow down.

I was at the bistro by nine to catch Andrea before her night started. We spotted each other at the same time.

—Hi, I—

—Where were you? she broke in. I thought we were having a meal this evening, and I waited for you at Happy's for two hours!

Two hours! She was reaching a boil. I tried again.

—I—

—You didn't tell me anything different. Her seething personality ignited the fire. *Get thee away from me, you infidel!*

I tried again.

—I—

—You don't need to say anything. Go!

I walked away without looking back. Her flaming-dragon breath could have made me into toast if I had looked. To this day, I cannot figure out what had gone wrong, what I had said, or where Happy's was.

Mother Mary Ann Dressed in Calico

Every soldier saluted her as she passed. Those who were at leisure relieved her of her burden and bore it to its destination. To the entire Army of the West, she was emphatically Mother Bickerdyke.

On a Sunday in June 1861, Mary Ann Bickerdyke had arrived at her church in Galesburg, Illinois. She knew life was a lonely place if you didn't have God in your heart. Her husband's recent death was making her life a challenge. Bowing her head, she prayed for guidance. Her friend Evelyn entered the hall and sat beside her.

—Good morning, Mary, she said in her soft voice.

—And good morning to you also, Mary Ann said with a smile. It's so nice this morning. Robins, my favorite birds, woke me up this morning.

Their chirping before sunrise is so refreshing. Then a wonderful walk down Water Street this morning, and I purposely did not go by Hope Cemetery. I need to make these small changes in my life.

Knowing her friend's loss just four months before, Evelyn was cautious about her comments.

—Mary, I'm delighted you took the path to church as you did away from his grave. I want only the best for you, and I pray for you.

—Thank you. I have a desire to help others because this civil war is horrible with all the human suffering. I want to help.

—I'm anxious for Pastor Beecher to read the letter he received about the wounded men we have in Cairo who need assistance. Mary, please. I'm sorry for you losing Robert, and I want the best for you. If that is what you want to do, I'll support you all I can.

But she was concerned that Mary Ann was reacting to her feelings, not from a true desire to provide help.

The Brick Congregational Church service started. The women listened as the choir sang. The pastor read a letter by a local man that told of the poor conditions at the military camp at Cairo, Illinois, where several hundred men from Galesburg were stationed, and the desperate need for volunteer help in the military camps there. The pastor also stated that President Lincoln asked for nurses and doctors to care for Northern militia during the civil war. Mary Ann Bickerdyke heard the plea.

—Mary Ann, do you mind if I walk home with you? Evelyn asked. Mary Ann replied with a nod. Evelyn was also a single woman, having lost her husband early in their marriage; therefore, no children. She had decided to remain single as it was God's will, not hers.

They walked slowly, occasionally looking at the many flowerbeds.

—Oh, this is so nice, Mary Ann said. God gives us this beauty to see, and I have decided to answer the call for help. She slowed her walk to a crawl. I will travel the 350 miles to Cairo to look at the army camp. Would you care to go with me, Evelyn?

Evelyn closed her eyes for several seconds searching for the correct response. She decided this journey would be good for her also.

—Yes, I will go with you. I will also notify the pastor so we can transport the supplies.

During that month, Galesburg's citizens donated $500 worth of supplies. The church arranging for a load of clothing, medical supplies, and food to Cairo to go with the women. Mary Ann put her household in order for a prolonged absence; her two sons were to live with a relative as she had volunteered for the war.

It took several days to get to Cairo by rail. The women had never ridden a train before and weren't prepared for the ride.

—Oh Evelyn, this train feels like a wagon going downhill with the horses running scared.

Mary Ann didn't have a scared look on her face; it was more one of apprehension.

—We're moving so fast. I look at a fence and before I know it, we are at the other end. I do hope no animals get in the way.

—Sir, Evelyn asked a conductor. We are moving so terribly fast. How can you possibly spot an animal and stop to not hit them?

—Ma'am, we have a device on the engine called a cowcatcher. It nudges a cow or other animal out of the way. 'Course, going twenty mile per hour, it's a pretty good nudge, replied the smiling conductor.

Dr. Woodward met the train and was surprised at the amount of baggage and supplies the two women had brought. It more than overloaded his carriage. He had to make second and third trips to convey everything. Dr. Woodward had assumed Mary Ann would come alone and only to bring supplies, view the Cairo camp, and leave that day.

Before they reached the camp, Mary Ann and Evelyn smelled a stench similar to corn silage spoiling. It was a rancid, putrid odor. They looked at each other. They knew the smell was the hospital camp.

The camp setup was essentially five tents each over a shallow pit. In the pit were cots for three men and a half-dozen more men lying on a bed of straw but mostly dirt. It appeared to have been in place since the tents had been set up about two weeks earlier. The straw was dirty and freely coated with vomit, urine, excrement, pus, and blood-clotted rags. Flies, lice, and maggots crawled over the men still wearing tattered battle clothes. The only person in charge appeared to be a man who was injured but not as badly as those inside the tent. He sat outside and passed a ladle of water inside, but that was only if a person in pain could ask for it.

—I just pull the dead out and let 'em put a new one in. I ain't here to help, he said.

Mary Ann asked Doctor Woodward if he could give these people better help.

—I'm too junior in this unit to get help from anyone, the doctor said. He hung his head in despair.

Mary Ann and Evelyn talked. They saw one solution was to get the men motivated by offering them incentives.

—There are no women here to cook. They'd want a good meal, Evelyn deduced. What if I went back toward Cairo, got some chickens, garden vegetables, and coffee and cooked a real good meal? You could get them to clean up here. These guys don't deserve these conditions.

—No they don't. I see some old barrels over there. Maybe I can get those guys by the campfire to split them in half for a bath for everyone. Get some good lye soap if you can, Evelyn. This Camp Hell needs a deliverance from evil so we can rename it Camp Hope.

—I'll do my best. I can get that good doctor to take me to town. It will be very hard otherwise.

—He will when I tell him to do it. He doesn't want to be or seem to know who is in charge, so I'll order him.

—That's the spirit! Mary Ann announced as Evelyn affirmed the new commander of the system.

The horse and cart left. Mary Ann walked toward six soldiers by a small, smoky campfire masking the odor of rotting flesh. She acted as if she wanted to watch the fire as they were doing. No one said hello other than a token glance at this woman dressed in a calico dress with a Shaker bonnet.

—You guys had lunch yet? Mary Ann asked. She received grunts that she interpreted as both yeses and nos. They were reacting as if they were snails. My cooking last Sunday smelled better than this. I sure could use another chicken dinner like the one I had. And those baked potatoes with butter and rolls and coffee like my mother taught me. She nudged the guy next to her. Do you hear my stomach grumbling? she asked in a humorous way as a signal to the others. They stopped stirring the fire with sticks. Mary Ann knew she had their attention.

—Well, I'll try to roll that barrel over this way and see if I can figure out how to make a dinner table. Maybe make a bathtub for those injured people in the tents. They would like that chicken dinner. I'll go over here and move it—

She moved toward the barrel. Three men looked at each other. One stood.

—I'll give you a hand for some of that chicken dinner.

Others felt hunger pangs for a woman-cooked meal and offered their help as well.

—Why thank you, guys. My name is Mary Ann Bickerdyke from Galesburg, Illinois. The other lady with me, Evelyn, has gone to town to get some vittles, and we'll have a real good chicken dinner for you. All we ask is for you to help us clean these tent sites. Your bellies will be full tonight. If anyone is a cook, I'll make him the camp cook. The doctor here has graciously agreed that I'll be in charge. We'll call this a tent camp, and we will help you. And for your information, my camp cooks will be second in charge.

A murmur of agreement met her words.

A woman in camp who got others talking attracted other men moping around their campfires. She spoke of making it a better camp, and they were inspired to help. Dr. Woodward did not know that he, by her saying so, had agreed to Mary Ann's taking over the hospital camp.

—Oh, and please find shovels. These tents need all that moldy straw and filthy dirt removed. These empty barrels cut in half can make bathtubs so I can give the injured baths. These seriously injured men deserve better beds. I cannot get their medical care to work without them being fed the same delicious chicken dinner you'll have. Would you agree with me?

The gathered men grinned and nodded. She saw they would work with her. Several men adjusted their clothes to make themselves more presentable with a woman in their midst.

—Put those big kettles with water over the fires, and the chickens will be making the best gumbo you've had since you enlisted, she said.

Mary Ann had given them vigor and enthusiasm. They willingly did as she asked. Evelyn returned from town with a carriage of food. Men rushed to remove all the provisions.

—Mary Ann! My, I am so surprised by all these guys pushing one another aside to unload the carriage. You really lit their fuse. Look at all those kettles of water being warmed and the barrels now looking like bathtubs. What have you not done, if I may ask?

—For now, I don't know, Mary Ann said as she gazed at the activity.

—I'm afraid this will be a long process. It will involve doctors and medicine and cleanliness. She sighed and shook her head. The enormity of the task of making the camp the first hospital camp raced through her mind. This is only one camp with many wounded. What's going on at the others? There may be many more like this, with no care for the wounded.

Some of the men in the straw beds objected to the women talking with them of taking their bloody and torn clothes off so they could be bathed.

—We're going to give you a nice bath, put clean clothes on you, and feed you a very nice chicken dinner, Mary Ann told a soldier in the tent who had had his arm severed days earlier.

—Ma'am, you can't take my clothes. I'll have nothing to wear. And, and I can't move very well. I'm so weak, he said.

—That is why we are here for you, Evelyn responded. We'll take these torn, dirty clothes off for you and replace them with better clothes and bathe you. We will be careful.

—Careful? My wife finds out you stripped me to the skin and touched me I'll never be able to enter her home! No ma'am.

—Mister, you are getting a very bad infection, Mary Ann said. If you don't let us bathe you, you could die and won't see anyone or anything. As volunteer nurses, we respect your privacy.

He realized his dilemma and agreed a bath was needed. The reward was going to be a chicken dinner, and Evelyn agreed to feed him. Other men were not so opposed to having a bath. They thanked Evelyn and called her Mother. Mary Ann treated them like her sons.

After eating the chicken, vegetables, and coffee, the men had settled down and were talking to one another, so unlike the camp that Mary Ann and Evelyn had entered that afternoon. Then, it had been a ghost town with tumbleweeds, but at that point, men were talking and laughing. One soldier's mouth harp added music to the atmosphere. Evelyn heard the tune, looked around, and spotted a man smiling. She asked him to dance to the ditty. Even with a wounded arm, he rose, and they jigged.

Mary Ann found another soldier to dance with. Soldiers began cutting in, and it was only when the harp player was winded that the dancing stopped. It was a night at the Cairo tent camp no one had ever seen.

Some men lying in straw beds heard the music and became aware they were not in a bed waiting to die but to be helped by this woman. They tried humming with the music and began calling Mary Ann Mother, because she was caring for them and assisting in their healing.

Others quickly picked up the name Mother for her because of the way she cared for them.

It took days for Mother and Evelyn to transfer as many men as they could to the hospital in Cairo and make the tent camp better. That meant numerous trips for supplies, setting up cooks with equipment, and getting some of the soldiers to manage the camp and return it to military order.

Mary Ann was asked to be a matron at the Cairo hospital. She wanted to but declined. She felt many more tent camps needed her first. She moved to another camp and saw the same terrible conditions as she had feared. Mother Bickerdyke imposed her system of order and relief. One of the surgeons saw her wearing a soft slouch hat with a gray overcoat of a rebel officer. She had given her blanket shawl to some poor fellow who had needed it.

—Report to me when you have this person stabilized, Mother yelled to no one in particular. The surgeon quizzically looked at her giving an order. In the middle of the camp, fires beneath kettles had hot soup ready. Evelyn was dispensing it along with crackers, tea, whiskey, water, and other refreshments to the shivering and wounded men.

—Where did you get these big kettles? an officer asked.

Evelyn looked at him but didn't answer. He watched her feeding the wounded men and cleaning and temporarily dressing their wounds.

—Ma'am, you are laboring here as a camp manager and a medical person. May I inquire under whose authority you are working?

—I have received my authority from the Lord God Almighty. Have you anything that ranks higher than that? she asked. She was a volunteer nurse who was caring for the wounded.

As she had seen at many other camps, the wounded were essentially expected to care for themselves. If their wounds were minor, they were expected to deal with them. If their wounds were major, the loss of a limb or their vision, there was the implied sentiment of "Sorry about your injury. Nice knowing you."

Many of the soldiers were disabled. Mary Ann was determined to treat them as best she could. She moved to the Cairo hospital, where she had been appointed matron. The surgeon who had appointed her was skilled and competent, but he had a bad attitude toward others not being of his ancestry. During Mary Ann's first day there, they got into a dispute regarding the care of wounded. He preferred minimum care, which also meant minimal food. He viewed his hospital money allotment as meant for the medical attendants, not for those who were dying.

Mary Ann Bickerdyke saw it differently. The wounded weren't dying until they did. In the meantime, they were to receive nutritious food, fruit, and medicine, as much as they needed. They were to be bathed and cared for. The medical staff was eating more than they should have and not monitoring patients as they should have. Her motherly attitude was coming out. No one could stop her caring.

Mother realized supplies, clothes, and delicacies sent to her for the sick and wounded were mysteriously disappearing. She thought the thieves were some of the personnel she depended on to care for the wounded. She threatened action against the accused. The sick were confined to their beds, so who else could have been the thieves?

Mary Ann often walked the halls to see how well the injured were being cared for. On one night stroll, she caught a male ward attendant dressed in clothes that had been sent to her. She seized him by the collar and sat with him in the cafeteria until breakfast. She disrobed him down to his pantaloons in the presence of the patients.

—Now, you rascal, let's see what you'll steal next!

To find out who was stealing the food, she came up with a ruse. She mixed a vomit-inducing powder she had bought at a drug store with stewed peaches she had cooked in the kitchen. She told the head cook she wanted to leave them on the table overnight to cool. She went to her room.

She didn't have to wait long. The sounds of the thieves' suffering soon reached her ears. Mary Ann went in and saw cooks, waiters, stewards, and ward attendants suffering from the emetic.

—Peaches didn't settle with you? My, my, she said with hands on hips. What some people will do.

Governor Harvey of Wisconsin was visiting the field where the Battle of Shiloh had occurred at Savannah, Tennessee, and the hospitals there to learn the wants and the condition of the soldiers from his state. He had a staff of volunteer surgeons and ten tons of numerous sanitary supplies. He saw every sick and wounded Wisconsin soldier and gave them all the medical attention and sanitary supplies they needed.

The governor was satisfied that he had done all in his power and happy he had been permitted to do so much good. He wondered what to do with the five tons of stores remaining; he didn't trust the surgeons in charge at Savannah. He turned over the stores to Mrs. Bickerdyke.

He had witnessed her efficiency, and he had spoken with those who worked with her. He was convinced he could trust her but no one else. The surgeon was instructed that these supplies would be in Mary Ann's custody.

After the governor returned to Wisconsin, Mary Ann began to suspect that her supplies were being sidetracked for the private uses of a certain surgeon's mess. She resolved to stop that. She entered the surgeon's tent just before dinner and discovered a great variety of the jellies, wines, and other comforts belonging to her stores. She took the evidence, went to the levee, took a boat to the Pittsburg Landing, and met with General Grant. Within twenty-four hours, the surgeon was under arrest. The other surgeons did not interfere with her or her stores after that. The sick and wounded rejoiced to find that their faithful friend had won such a victory.

—Mother, the surgeon of the fourth ward hasn't made his appearance, and the special diet list has yet to be made out. No one has had breakfast, a young ward attendant told her one morning.

—Haven't had their breakfasts? I have let them down! They must be fed immediately! Mother was enraged. She clenched her fists.

She and Mary Livermore filled the tin pails and trays with coffee, soup, gruel, toast, and other food. Mother sent six men ahead of her, shouting instructions about what to check. Mother handed Mary a large pail of hot soup and was carrying a pail of similar size. Mary, who was beholding the commotion, heard Mother's distinct, authoritarian voice.

—Come alive, Mary Livermore! Be useful! Help these men!

As they were laboring, the surgeon of the ward came in looking as if he had just risen from sleeping off a drunk. Mary Ann became Genghis Khan.

—You miserable, drunken scalawag! She shook her finger at him threateningly.

—What do you mean by leaving these hurting, suffering men with nothing to eat?

He tried to explain but was cut off.

—Not a word, sir! Leave this hospital. I will see you gone in three days.

Mary Ann made such charges against him that he was dismissed from the service in less than a week. The surgeon complained to General Sherman about the injustice she had done him.

—I have been grossly belied, and wrongful charges had been made against me, which I can prove false, he declared.

—Who was your accuser? General Sherman asked. Who made the charges?

—Why, it was that spiteful old woman, Mrs. Bickerdyke.

—Well, then, if it was she, I can't help you. She has more power than I do. She outranks me, Sherman said.

The story of Mother Bickerdyke's exploits in the Savannah Hospital preceded her in the army. She was a special individual to wounded soldiers. Those who did not care to perform their obligations quickly learned Mary Ann Bickerdyke could not be forced or frightened.

The Sanitary Commission had set up a depot of supplies, and Mary Ann was allowed to make her orders without any problem. She was known for her no-nonsense, careful use of supplies. Her sense of cleanliness was the equivalent of godliness.

Major General John "Black Jack" Logan met Mary Ann for the first time late one night after a battle. He was lying in his tent, casually stretching out after having been on horseback most of the day. He observed a lone figure with a lamp crisscrossing the battlefield.

—Corporal! he hollered.

—Sir?

—Have an orderly go into the battlefield and capture the person out there. Bring him to me.

The orderly returned with Mary Ann, who was wearing a calico dress.

—What do you think you are doing on a battlefield? You're supposed to be at the tent camp tending the wounded.

—I couldn't rest until I had scouted the field to be sure no living man remained. I do not want one life that could have been saved to have been lost. But thank you, General, for being attentive to activities.

—I do care that our weapons and uniforms should not be used to infiltrate our side, so we have to be vigilant, the general said.

—My calico dress is recognized by the Confederates who are scouting the field for their men also. We have a shared agreement to honor the wounded and dead. Why can't the Union army also recognize the South when both of you are not fighting?

—Madam, this army fights to win battles, and it is not a gentlemen's fistfight. I will allow you to be there at night, but no collaboration with them about our intentions or you will be arrested for spying. Understand me?

She did not blink.

—Yes I do. I am there only for the wounded.

The story was picked up by the press and contributed to her growing folk-hero status. After that, General Logan often confided in her about events. He did not call her mother, but he considered her as his mother. He depended on her to provide for his men.

—Lieutenant, ask Mrs. Bickerdyke to drop by my office this evening, please.

—Sir, did you mean Mother Bickerdyke?

—Yes of course I meant her!

Many hours later, General Logan was lying in bed, lantern off.

—General, Mother is here. Do you wish to see her yet?

Groaning, he relit the lantern as she entered his office—his tent. Her clothes were splattered with blood. Her face reflected her fatigue.

—Well, you just done for the night now? he asked factiously.

—The wounded die day or night unless we provide relief. She was curt. What was your question?

The general was used to being in charge, not being questioned. He was at a loss for words. He had been on innumerable battlefields. He had seen war's carnage.

—I beg your pardon, Mrs. Bickerdyke. You are dismissed. I have no question for you.

Mother turned and left.

The war's western frontier involved various skirmishes at sites determined by the battle line. A captain was moving his troops in Illinois toward Fort Donelson, Tennessee. He was riding with a very stiff back in his saddle, his lips glued shut. Mary Ann, who was working with nurses at the Corinth Hospital, learned a brigade was nearing the hospital. She invited the captain to halt his exhausted men so she and her staff could feed them, but he refused.

The captain was determined to get to the fort as quickly as he could. He was leading his men in a fast-step march as an example of a true officer following orders. The only sound was the creaking of cannon carriages being pulled and the scuffle of many shoes marching until a deep, bull-moose voice like that of a retired sergeant was heard

—Company, halt!

The voice was a new one to the troops. The men slowed to a stop. Their bafflement was replaced with delight when they herd Evelyn's softer, feminine voice.

—Mess call!

A group of women led by Mary Ann was quickly serving as a tin cup brigade offering bread, fruit, water, soup, and coffee.

The captain was astounded that his troops had been stopped by the call of "Halt!" and had been disrupted by a mess call. Military drills were second fiddle to that feminine voice.

By the time anyone admitted Bickerdyke had roared the order to halt, all had been served the only food they would have for two days.

—Sergeant, who gave the command to halt?

—Sir, it was the lady who invited you to stop the men for a bite to eat. Before I could countermand the order, the other woman hollered "Mess call," and there was no way to restore military order, sir.

The captain was seething that women had in three seconds trumped two weeks of military orders and training.

—Please obtain some of that food for me so I can make a report on this ... this mutiny!

It was reported that the captain had obtained some food as evidence for his formal complaint to the major general. Further reports were that the captain's test involved his eating the evidence.

The formal reprimand Mary Ann received brought no firm promise from her of reform other than not bellowing as she had done in ranks. That had not been a properly given order.

Mother was frugal. She saw that the clothes taken off the wounded were routinely collected for burning or burial, a waste of clothing in near-perfect condition. She wrote to the Sanitary Commission in Chicago for washing machines, a clothes press, and portable kettles. She received the authority and monitored the laundering of all the formerly repugnant garments. They were packed and came again into use for other battles.

This work made Mother Bickerdyke even more active in hospitals and battlefield camps. Her assembly of portable kettles, washing machines, clothing collectors, and two-horse wagon ambulances were her tools wherever she went. They cared for the wounded and sick. They wanted to help save lives and send wounded soldiers home.

Mary Ann was later assigned to hospital ships on the Ohio and Mississippi Rivers on the war's frontier. Supplies were made available to her as she ensured the wounded were promptly cleaned, dressed in clean clothes, and nourished by food.

—As the surgeon on this ship, we needed only to administer medicine and dress wounds. Her care of the wounded is amazing, stated a surgeon on an Ohio River ship.

—The wounded, needing her help, will each holler for her, begging for her assistance and care. She treated every one of them as her sons.

General Grant had given her a pass anywhere within the lines of his area of responsibility—into all camps and hospitals, past all pickets, with authority to draw on any quartermaster in his department even as it grew for army wagons to transport sanitary or hospital stores. She held this pass until the end of the war.

The Sanitary Commission authorized her to draw on its depot of stores at Memphis, Cairo, or Chicago for anything needed for the boys. She never abused the trust given her. With rigorous conscientiousness, she devoted all she had and was to the cure and comfort of the soldiers in hospital without favoritism or partiality.

While they had no doubt that the good woman made legitimate use of the money and articles, the officials of the commission often objected to her methods of transactions. She was often asked to give an accounting of why supplies, equipment, and vouchers were submitted with no dates, but she had no idea of where she would be the next day let alone that afternoon.

Bills, notes, and vouchers in her hands were often paid by funds raised among and by her friends. The commission believed she should be sustained in her wonderful work even though she was irregular in her daily procedures. Her situations often dictated what to do, where it should be done, and how to handle it.

Churches in Illinois that learned of her pleas for the welfare of the boys who needed it were continually sending medicine, clothes, bandages, and food to wherever she was. Among the articles sent her at one time were two very elegant, embroidered nightdresses trimmed with lace and ruffles. They were a gift from some dear friends; Mary Ann had some concerns about bartering them for goods as she did other garments. Returning with the items she had received in exchange for her unessential clothing, she spotted a railroad boxcar train by a crossing.

She began to explore it; that was her manner of retrieving items she needed for the troops. Inside a car, she found two wounded soldiers who were hitching a ride home on medical leave. She saw flies on their unhealed and undressed wounds. They were hungry, discouraged, depressed, and in bad medical conditions.

—The Lord knew what I would need, and He provided. These nightgowns were sent here for a purpose, she said. She washed and cleaned their wounds and tore the nightdresses into bandages.

—After I dress these wounds, I have socks and drawers for you guys, and I can make you shirts off the upper half of these nightgowns, just the thing. My sakes, but this is lucky!

Andy looked at Bucky and then at Mary Ann.

—Ma'am, no offense to you, but a woman's nightgown? No thank you.

Bucky nodded in agreement.

—We got shot in these here dirty, tattered shirts. They have a ripe smell of being on our backs for two months. I'd rather that than go home in a woman's nightgown!

—Please, boys, listen to me. Nightgowns or nightshirts, what's the difference other than a word? These will be softer to your wounds, are much cleaner, and your wounds will heal quicker. If anybody says anything, tell them you jerked 'em off the back of Confederates and the folks will think a heap sight more of you for it.

That made sense. They donned their new shirts.

The battles continued. Mother Bickerdyke's efforts increased. She knew most camps didn't adequately care for men brought in from the battlefield. She tried to impress upon the Sanitary Commission the importance of being ready with ambulances and supply storehouses.

At times, wounded Confederates were in her hands, but she set aside any anger she felt. When she saw a wounded soldier on a battlefield, she became his mother whether he was wearing blue or grey.

She was equally effective on her occasional speaking forays for the Sanitary Commission. One day toward the end of the war, she was invited to speak with the women of Henry Ward Beecher's church in Brooklyn.

Mrs. Laymane began the meeting with a remarkable opening.

—Ladies, I am very happy to introduce to you today a woman from Illinois. Depending on whom you ask, she is known as Mother or the Cyclone in Calico. She cares very much for the troops be they Northern or Southern. A wounded soldier needs the care a mother can provide. The Cyclone in Calico finds and provides needed items. I am also very proud to welcome her assistant, Evelyn. They will talk about the many field hospitals they helped establish for medical care. I present to you Mary Ann Bickerdyke.

Mary Ann stood to the applause of the fifty women.

—Halt! she said when the applause refused to die down.

—Halt! the women shouted and laughed.

Mary Ann had their attention.

—Thank you. Thank you. Evelyn is a great person working with me, and I do appreciate all the help she has given the troops. Not just help with me but for the boys. I am pleased to be here with you not just to give a sort of missionary's report on how well the teaching of God's word is going. I am here to talk to you as a mother. I will tell you about the absolute defilement of human life after a battle that I am finding. Do you use a bandage when your son has cut his arm, or do you pull his sock off, cut a swath of cloth from it, and tie it over the wound?

Do you know that is what I have had to do time after time near these battlefields?

Mary Ann walked over to Evelyn.

—Evelyn and I and other nurses had to bind the arm and leg stumps of many amputees with old cloth bags. Mary Ann was standing before them holding her arms in a praying position. Or any piece of cloth not covered by blood or body pieces.

A gasp came from the audience. Several women covered their mouths and rushed to the exits.

—I ask for your help. In this day and age, 1864, I have to beg people for rags to wipe the bloody face of a mother's son. You have items and material we can use. Soldiers fighting for yours rights need what you have. Stand up where you are right now! Stand up!

They stood as if in a spell, not knowing what to expect.

—You ladies have very pretty dresses on that I would love to own. Your dresses have many petticoats. Lift your dress and drop one of your petticoats to the floor for me. They will provide the clean cloth instead of a cloth bag. The soldiers will be thankful for what you have donated, and I'm sure you will know they will help prevent infection and give the boys the cleanliness they need. They will save lives.

The collected garments filled three trunks. Within weeks, Mary Ann Bickerdyke was using pieces of petticoats to bandage terrible wounds of patients in field hospitals.

Upon General Lee's surrender at Appomattox, Virginia, on April 9, 1865, Mary Ann Bickerdyke realized the fighting had stopped but the soldiers were still hurting, possibly for the rest of their lives. Her concerns were for the wounded who depended on her.

In the summer of 1865, Mary Ann and Evelyn were discussing the war over dinner.

—Well, it's over, but I'm worried about all these soldiers hurting so much. Wounds don't go away just because the shooting has stopped, Mary Ann said. Nor do the families return to normal when all those people with missing limbs are home and cannot work, Evelyn said. Oh I pity the reality. Mary Ann, do you think we could establish a hospital or something to help care for them? I know the Sanitary Commission will close now with the war being over, but the boys will need help for forever. They're injured and hurting. I guess you and I, Evelyn, are the only ones who truly care. I have heard of another woman, Clara Barton, who is active in caring for the boys in the Eastern states. I hope she cares for the boys like we do.

—Evelyn, I received a letter from General Sherman. He asked us to Washington, DC to participate in the parade down Pennsylvania Avenue. Do you want to go? I am going only to pull on the ties of those guys at the Capitol and let them know the wounded soldiers need help.

—Mary Ann, if it's okay with you, I'm so tuckered out. Traveling is about the last thing I want to do. The ambulances brought in more from Missouri, and I want to care for them. Evelyn had been through four years of toil. And another ambulance was arriving.

—I know what you're saying. I know you and the other nurses will handle it. I have to get to Washington and plead for the care the boys need.

Mary Ann met General Sherman after a train ride that had made her feel like a cannon ball in flight.

—Ah, Mary Ann, so nice to see you here in Washington. We have reserved seats on the reviewing stand for the parade.

—Thank you, General. I trust we will also visit the hospital here so the boys will know that Mother is here. I also want to speak with some senators after the parade about their—

—Please, Mary Ann. This is a parade review to celebrate! I'd planned we could have seats at the state dinner tonight, listen to music, and relax.

—Relax? With thousands of boys wounded for life you want to relax? I will have you know, sir, my relaxing during the parade will be at the end of the parade when I thank them, as many as I can speak to.

Mother was riled. After greeting the troops who had marched, she went to the hospital to greet the boys confined to bed. She wanted to encourage them with the words of a mother.

On March 21, 1866, Mary Ann felt that her work for the army was finished, so she resigned from the Sanitary Commission. She wasn't paid a cent for all her hard work; her five years of service had been voluntary.

For the rest of her life, she worked to help former soldiers and their families impacted by homelessness or plagues. Kansas residents never forgot what she had done in regard to the 1874 locust plague. Due to the assistance she had gotten for them, they hung her portrait in the state capitol.

And medical personnel in Illinois didn't forget her help during the war. A sizeable amount of money was contributed for a monument in Illinois to honor her innumerable work for people.

Mary Ann Ball Bickerdyke passed away peacefully on November 8, 1901, in Kansas. She was buried next to her husband in Galesburg, Illinois. A statue of her was erected in Galesburg. A hospital boat and a liberty ship, the *Mary Bickerdyke*, were named after her.

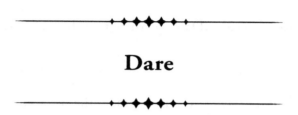

Dare

Her name was Daniela, but she loved her nickname, Dare. We hit it off while we were in a social chat room. I used the chat name Andy Panda; my real name was Andrew Beare. Our emails became more frequent, and phone calls led to our meeting at a quaint restaurant with fabric flowers on tables.

—Tell me why you like Dare as a nickname.

—I love how it sounds. I like to think of myself as a female daredevil, so it's Dare. It's so alluring. Dare me and maybe I'll do something naughty for you. Don't you think it's cute, Andy?

I thought about her proclamation as I watched her spoon beans out of her chili.

—Yeah, it's cute. I dare you to go to the counter and tell the waitress there's an insect in your soup.

Dare walked to the counter holding her bowl.

—Ma'am, I have an insect in my chili. Can you replace it for me?

The waitress looked at Dare and then in the bowl. She tried to mask her smirk.

—I don't see the fly, so it must be under the surface. If you have an insect in your soup, the chili can't be vegetarian.

Dare's jaw dropped. She returned to the table as the waitress watched with a gotcha smile. But Dare kept a bounce in her walk and a forced smile on her face. She implied that no trick had happened to her. I'd seen the counter action and had heard their conversation.

—Everything okay? I innocently asked.

—Oh yes. Sometimes I eat meat. I'll see if I can find one in my bowl for you, Andy.

It was a few weeks before Christmas. We were living in Hagerstown, Maryland. We were sitting on the couch holding hands. I had a dare for her that had been stewing in my mind.

—Okay, Dare, here's an idea. January is in a couple of weeks, and to welcome in the New Year, we can join the Polar Bear Club on the Potomac River at noon at Williamsport Park. Not quite skinny-dipping but close to it. We'll let people see us with others getting the blood chilled out of us. It'll be wild.

I saw a gleam in her eyes. She recognized a dare when she heard one. She was getting excited about it.

—Oh yes, let's do it! That would be more than cool, and I want to. I'll wear my string bikini. How I wish January were tomorrow.

She was totally jazzed at the idea.

On January 1, Dare woke at sunup and pulled my pillow from under my head to rouse me. She was already in her string bikini. We had celebrated New Year's Eve at a friend's house and hadn't gotten home until three. It was just past seven. I was supposed to be as excited as she was to get up, slip on my swimsuit, and wait for five hours for the noon river plunge.

I turned on the TV and saw it was sunny outside. The temperature was eight, but the wind chill made it five degrees. Winds from the west at six miles per hour. A perfect day and temperature to raise goose bumps on goose bumps.

Dare paced the house, her anxiety level high. She wanted to get going.

—Why don't you shovel the sidewalk? I asked her. Or wash the car? No! Forget that. We'd never get the car door open. Dare, just go outside and sit in the sun. Your tan could use an improvement.

She looked at her skin, rubbed her arm, and nodded.

—You're right. I'll get some sun.

She went to the closet for I thought a coat. Nope. A lawn chair. Me and my big mouth. And her believing her tan had faded.

Through the window, I watched the charade of her sitting in the chair and soaking up eight-degree sunshine. I saw a blue SUV speeding down the road slow down and back up to view the bikini-clad woman sunning her goose bumps.

Dare came in sometime later. I expected to see her shivering.

—That was a really cool idea, Andy. I never imagined sitting in the sun in January in Maryland could give me such a feeling of nature talking to me. It's a rush!

I realized then that I'd never understand the logic of Dare.

We traveled to the river one hour before the event. She wanted to get there early. She had a long coat over her bikini. I swear, a handkerchief could have covered more skin than her bikini did. I was wearing pants, sweater, long-sleeved shirt, gloves, hat, and coat over my swimsuit. I knew I couldn't chicken out of the adventure. I put on a stoic face. I was going for it.

The dash to the water was scheduled for noon. Dare wanted to jump in twenty minutes early to warm up, but she stayed in the car. She looked around to see if she knew anyone. Yup, there was Bubba. She stripped out of her coat, jumped out, and ran to him. He was sitting in his truck with an open window, and Dare was standing outside chatting as if it were eighty degrees. Their conversation ended. She walked back. Cameras were clicking. Not at icebergs in the river. At her.

—Is Bubba going swimming with us? I asked.

—Naw, he said he came to watch the morons jump in. I'm nippy now, but I'll give them a show for their money.

Fifteen minutes before the plunge, we were standing outside in swimsuits.

—Dare, we can tell everyone we're in swimsuits to show our support. That's all! I pleaded.

—You! You *dared* me, and I'll be damned to pretend at this point. You got petrified Rocky Mountain oysters or what?

—No. They're just slow moving, I murmured.

—You want me to give them a kick-start?

—No. I'll get them started.

—What*ever*, she snapped, looking away.

Everyone had a blanket or coat on. Everyone but Dare. Just bare skin and a bikini. The event officials informed everyone to stay with his or her partner at all times. If a problem came up, yell to the beach for help. Dare was sneering under her breath at all the advice.

—Okay, people, line up in pairs along the shore. Drop your blanket, grab your partners' hands. Ready?

The whistle signaled. Dare yanked me into the river. The water's first touch on me wasn't bad, but when my head went under, I felt as if I'd touched an electric fence. It was numbing. It made me realize I wasn't an ice cube meant to jump into a glass of tea. This was the other way around. The Potomac River was chilling the dingbat out of me. I wrenched my hand from hers and raced for shore. I hoped she was right behind me. Nope. She was standing in the water, rinsing her hair, and watching icebergs float downstream. She slowly walked the twenty feet to shore, splashing water on herself as she came ashore.

I was shaking like a leaf. I was freezing. I had the blanket about as tight as I could make it. Dare was still knee deep in the river.

—Please Dare, get over here with me in this blanket so I can warm up. Please!

Oh no. Dare ignored me. She stood around thirty seconds more for photos before walking to our car. She paused with the door open as if to air the car out. I had dashed to the car and sat there shaking like Jell-O and Dare had to air the car.

I was about to drive off and let her aerate her derriere by walking back to our place. She finally got in.

—Ah, that was relaxing and so different. It feels like when you let the air out of a tire and put fresh air in. The tire feels new.

How would a tire know if it contains fresh air?

—Hey, let's stop at the Shoppe. I'm thirsty, she said.

I hadn't said a word to her since she stopped airing the car out. My lips and the mind to use them were still in a semi-frozen state.

She was still in her bikini with no cover. I gave her two dollars, and she went in. Ten people eating dropped their fries and watched a summer's vision saunter to the counter. With her hair frozen in place, she asked for a large drink. Cooks and burger boys ignored the fry alarms as they watched this Wonder Woman. The sign on the door read "No shirt, No shoes, No service." But rules were meant to be broken. Did she ever. She came out. Her thawed hair was dripping.

Her drink had lots of ice. I needed a tub of hot coffee to sit in and see if it had a bottom.

—Okay, Dare, you have everyone in shock. M-m-may we go home so I can get back to roo-room temperature? I'm really shivering and shaking bad. Please?

—What*ever*.

She acted as if she wanted to sip her drink and ride around.

Oh, can we—

A pause.

—Never mind. You wouldn't want to do that either.

Lady, you got that right.

We reached home, and I raced to the door. I shook so much that the key had problems finding the lock.

—Here, let me, she said.

I ran to the bathroom and leaped into the hot shower. I jumped out screaming in pain. I found out my skin cannot go from frozen to boil that fast without nerves interceding. Dare came into the bathroom with a towel, telling me to lie on the bed. She gently massaged my body, returning it to room temperature. She was still in just her bikini.

Later, I was feeling better. We sat at the dining table. Dare at last had clothes on. I was in long sleeves and she was in short sleeves.

—Do you feel like going … she began. I gave her the female look.

—What*ever*, she said.

We stayed home that evening. I touched her skin. It was warm.

—Why didn't you get cold like I did? I still feel like permafrost.

—Silly! The water was not frozen as it was what, thirty-five degrees? The air was eight degrees. The water was much warmer.

—But thirty-five's cold!

—Andy, it's all logical and relevant, as Sherlock Holmes called it. Just think of it as pleasant, nice. Besides, my hair needed a good rinse. It was cute watching old people yelling and the young kids enjoying today.

By the following January, I had let my Polar Bear Club membership expire. You know who kept hers.

A Modern Love Story

As a single, young, twentyish, male paralegal for a national real estate company, my life was active in terms of paper shuffling but physically lame. My coworkers agreed that it was because I didn't do too much of anything other than sitting at a desk looking at property and sale documents. If the intern wasn't available, I'd go to the courthouse for property searches. As a course of action to keep my body in physical shape, I walked several miles every workday.

It was refreshing to hear the sounds of birds and view the wild plants along the park trail. It was an opportunity to leave work behind and relax—no concerns, letting my mind wander. Traffic noise was in the distance, and the air was fresh. In good weather, I was in the park. In bad weather, I'd go to the YMCA to exercise.

One day at the Y, while I was on the stepper, an agile woman took a walker near mine. I nodded a hello, and she returned it. *My God, look at her!* My heart palpitated at this Godiva. Her black hair, the way she carried herself, her smile as she used a machine that made me breathe heavily. *I must be dreaming.*

We started meeting on breaks and had brief conversations over the month. I didn't remember much of what we talked about. All I remembered was her name, Marie. Our encounters at the Y stopped when her membership expired.

In a city park near where I lived, a sidewalk circled the lake. I was sitting there on a park bench. Children were feeding the geese and ducks when a woman with a young child stopped. She sat on the other end of the bench and told the girl to go ahead and feed Daffy. Her voice sounded familiar. I looked and saw Marie.

—Daffy? I asked. Hi, Marie. Is that her favorite duck? I hadn't heard of a duck here having a name.

—Hi. Yes, Daffy. She likes all ducks, so when she asked me his name, I said Daffy.

—Your daughter can toss the corn really well. She looks about five.

—Annette is my sister's daughter. She's six. I often take her after school for walks or shopping so she won't be home alone. Her mother is a single parent and has to work two jobs, so I try to help. Do you come here to feed the ducks and geese?

—No. I like to watch the kids feeding them. I walk various places just to be outside before I go home.

I hoped to continue the conversation. Meeting her like that was a good time to get to know each other better. Particularly with the young girl having fun, feeding Daffy.

—Annette, we have to go now.

Without any other word or a look, they left. My smile turned to sealed lips as I watched them leisurely walk away. She never looked back. *Oh well. Nice try.*

Marie had had no wedding band. She was in her twenties and had a niece she liked making happy. Maybe she could make me happy.

Two months later, we met again. Fall was well underway. The oak leaves were losing their color. I was lost in thought sitting in the park and hadn't noticed the young child who had walked up to me

—Hi, she said.

—Hi, I said automatically. Then I noticed it was Annette. A woman was well behind Annette.

—Aunt Marie said she hoped you'd be here, Annette said.

I smiled and waved at Marie.

—I see you two have jackets on. Won't be long before Daffy flies south.

Marie started to comment, but Annette beat her to it.

—Oh no! Daffy lives here. We were here during the last snow, and I saw Daffy sitting on the ice, and he was shaking.

I asked why he was shaking, and she told me he stayed warm by shivering.

—Well, you know more about that stuff than I. Maybe so. Feeding Daffy today? I asked.

Marie sat on the other end of the bench. She gave her niece a small bag of bread pieces. The girl quickly moved to the water's edge.

—Please be careful, Annette, or Dale will have to jump in for you.

My eyes bulged.

—Um, my name's Larry.

She grinned. She looked down. She looked at me.

—I'm sorry. I forgot what you had said your name was. My name's Marie. I had to call you something.

—Glad to see you, Marie. Don't think it will be too much longer and my gloves will be needed every day.

—Yeah. We'll have to do some inside activity.

We looked at Annette as she talked.

—Maybe she'd like a dance class, she said.

—Maybe she'd like that. Don't you think she would prefer a sport? Say soccer at the Y? They do have a girls' winter indoor league. I think exercise at her age is beneficial for growth development. And it will help her become bigger in the—

—What are you, a *weirdo?* Marie jumped to her feet, hands on hips. No one will ever say such a thing to me about my niece, and you to think that is disgusting! Annette, she yelled. Come on. We're going.

I was open mouthed at her outburst.

—Her *motor* skills, Marie. That's all I was going to say. I spoke slowly. Development of her motor skills. I meant nothing else!

It dawned on me that it was how I had said it, not what I said.

—Oh.

A silent pause. She sat. Annette appeared. She was puzzled about the anger that had been in Marie's voice. Marie looked at me.

—Sorry. I'm a little edgy right now and just short on listening. Annette, I'd like to go. What do you say to a nice roast beef sandwich and hot chocolate?

I said bye to the duo as they walked off. Annette turned her head and smiled. I figured any further meeting was cancelled.

Winter was in full swing. The temps were in the twenties for the high. Some people considered that warm. I had long ago been into the bar and dance-floor scene and knew it was just a game room to confuse and enthuse. A virtual mine for prospectors of fools' gold. I had left it far behind for better places to meet women. Like the library, church, or gym.

I ran, lifted weights, and used the equipment at the Y two, three evenings a week, but the pleasure was eroding. I had no real goal for keeping fit other than to be doing something. I met several interesting women in the Y, but their real objective was not another person but staying in Hollywood shape, be noticed, and hope their activities on social networks would be the golden egg.

I volunteered to be a timer and scorekeeper at the Y. It was fascinating to watch the energized young kids. I often had to be reminded that I was a timer, not a cheerleader, and that I should focus on each game's continuity.

In one particularly contested basketball game, both teams tied for first place. Someone tapped my shoulder. I noticed it but continued my duties as the timer. Thirty seconds later, it occurred again. I looked. Marie nodded hello. I waved hello back and returned my attention to the game. I noticed that Annette was playing and doing great layups.

The game went into overtime. Marie, seated behind me, shouted louder. Or was I finally getting attuned to her voice? Sadly, Annette's team lost by one point after ten minutes of overtime.

After the loss, Annette went to the locker room. I still had one more game as the timer, but Marie stayed right behind me. She tapped on my shoulder during a timeout.

—I get excited watching the girls play basketball. I used to be a cheerleader, and I still get excited watching good plays. Hope you don't mind my use of your shoulder as a drum.

—Go ahead, I said. I like to see the action these kids put into the games. I smiled. *Maybe we can hit it off again like in the exercise room.*

We had a late-afternoon lunch at the mall later. Annette went to a game room as we sat nearby

—Are you calmed down now? Eating your sandwich, you were still in high gear, I said.

—I think so. Kids can really get me going. I sometimes remember when we were young and there were no outdoor sports in the winter other than at school. Did your school ever have donkey basketball?

—Donkey basketball? Donkeys can't play.

—Silly! Popular disc jockeys, local singers, and teachers would ride donkeys and make shots. It was just a comedy show. I was in elementary school and went to one. You don't remember?

—Sorry. My mind only remembers my dad complaining about gasoline costing ninety-nine cents a gallon. He swore he was going to start walking to work.

—Well, did he?

—Once. I remember him so bushed after he walked back that Mom had to bring him a TV dinner so he wouldn't have to get out of his lazy chair. We kids laughed so much seeing him eating and then falling asleep. Mom woke him up, and he went straight to bed. A friend gave him a ride to and from work after that day. God, that was funny.

We were laughing at that, remembering a time when we were young.

Annette had returned while we were talking about the past, so we began a casual walk around, viewing the displays. I noticed after Marie's pointing at a nice dress on sale that her hand was resting on my lower arm. I smiled at her and returned the gesture by gently holding her hand. It was a bonding moment.

But it was getting late. Marie had to take Annette home. She and I exchanged emails and cell numbers. I hugged her.

—I hope you had as good a day as I had. I like your company, I said.

—With you, yes I did, she said with a smile. The day was nice, but you are someone I am beginning to like. Have a pleasant evening.

We began to send each other tasteful jokes or pictures with an occasional R rating. I tried not to call too much and kept the calls cordial, funny. It became like a teenage dating thing between us—movies or dinners together. We agreed not rushing into things was right. We were just keeping each other company.

One day, I was riding with Marie after we'd completed a light workout at the Y. Our conversation had been jovial with talk about a video we'd seen of a deer in a grocery store that had slipped and slid around as it was trying to find a way out. One clip showed the deer running into and pushing a cart half-full of groceries for a bit.

—It would have been so funny if the deer had gotten out the door with the cart and the sheriff's deputy was in pursuit and lost track of the deer, she said. I agreed.

Another time, Marie and I were going to her place. She was driving fast, anxiously talking as she reached her residence.

—I'll be back in a moment, she said. She hurried inside. She returned after ten minutes in different clothes. I caught the scent of perfume. She seemed much more at ease.

—Sorry I took so long. I had to change into better clothes.

I discovered her anxiety was due to the fact she had reservations for us at the India Mongoose restaurant just outside town.

—I like their achars here, she told me.

—Why not? I'll have one.

I thought she had said *anchors* but didn't know it was a pickled fish or some game.

The bistro was pleasant, comfortable. Sitar music was playing in the background. She ordered first. I ordered the same. The conversation warmed up quickly with talk and jokes. We spent time looking at each other and holding hands.

Her laughter was infectious. *Where have I been to miss this cherub?* Wait! Two other women had started the same thing with me, but that had quickly flamed out both times.

We just about closed the restaurant. A quick hug ended the night, but I went home and felt happy to have spent the evening with her.

We arranged another date. She was okay with going to the Greek restaurant I liked, complete with music. We enjoyed a wonderful *sheftalia*. Marie had asked what it was. The waitress replied it was a well-seasoned sausage on pita. Marie was pleased with it.

We talked about her job as an account manager for a restaurant chain.

—Do you eat there often? If I could eat there for free, I would.

Marie looked at me in disbelief.

—You? You'd want to eat ice cream for breakfast or another dessert for a midnight meal?

—No. I think I'd rather eat regular than selling chips and expect that to be supper. I know some jobs do have drawbacks with the positives we have.

—Will you be at the Y next weekend? she asked.

—Yes. I'm the scorekeeper and timer for this season. With the basketball season over, they have indoor soccer for the kids.

We didn't stay late. I had to work the next day. Back at her door, she thanked me for a pleasant evening and gave me a hug and a slow kiss.

—I'll call tomorrow, okay? she asked.

—Right. I'll be waiting.

—Good evening, Larry. Had a busy day at work?

I fumbled with the phone. I'd gotten to it just before the answering machine took over.

—Hi! I was at the other end of the house when you called and had to make a mad dash to catch you. I was puffing from the dash. Today was busy. The company signed a big contract to develop the land by the interstate into a mall. They've been arguing over the terms for weeks.

—They? I thought you said it was buyer and seller threatening each other over details.

—Yeah, it was Davis and Hangerte. There's so much paperwork, signatures, and certified checks involved with these big-boy deals. I guess they need these things when the smallest bill in their wallet is a hundred.

—I'm grateful to have several twenties, Marie replied. Do they ever say how much money they make out of these sales?

—The real estate company or the seller?

—Your company.

—Well, the agent gets six-seven percent for a house. If it's like that for a company, that'd be … seven hundred thousand for a ten-million-dollar sale. It's no wonder real estate agents brag in sales ads about having had million-dollar years. Oh well. It's not me.

There was silence on the line as if each of us wondered what to say next.

—Lawrence, there's something I need to tell you.

She'd called me Lawrence. I considered the use of the proper first name was a signal of change one way or the other.

—I like you a lot, but I want to be sure.

Sure I can or sure she can?

—May I ask the purpose of your statement or—

I left a fill-in-the-blank sentence or a dangling participle for her.

—Larry? *Ahhh, a real name now.* When I'm with you, I feel different, I—I shouldn't be talking like this. I should talk with you face to face, not on the phone. I think phones often make talk sound too impersonal and cold. Let me just say thanks for an interesting talk about your day. Your voice does stuff to me. Goodnight, Larry.

—And a happy goodnight to you too. I enjoy our talks, and you're right. Talks face to face are more personal. I like you very much. I hope we can continue to be good friends. In fact, I'd like to be with you more.

—I think I would like that too. Bye, Larry.

—Bye, Marie.

It was like a reality movie we were the developers for and liked it. However, when Marie said she liked me but wanted to be sure, did that imply internal thinking about me or another guy, a rival? Then her other statement that a voice does stuff to her implied it was me. Moreover, I had many warm love thoughts about her.

Marie's sister had moved to another state, so Marie's visits with her niece became infrequent. Annette also wanted to spend her time with her friends. Marie adored her sister's daughter and cared for the child as if she were her own. The slowdown in their visitation left an empty spot in Marie's life. As a way to fill the empty spot, we were dining, going to movies, and dancing more before I got a clue as to what "sure" meant. We were at a nice restaurant having prime rib when she asked a loaded question. She kept looking down several times as if a question was near.

—Larry, we've been dating, what, three, four months? There's something I have to ask you.

I was silent, I had a feeling a nuclear bomb was about to hit. I sometimes feel fatalistic.

—You say you like me, but you don't show it. I try to be feminine with you, but you act like I'm supposed to make a pass. I did once, but you seemed tuned out. You acted indifferent, like it was a joke. I'm attracted to you, Larry, but if it's only me, I'm unsure of what's going on.

That was a nine on the Richter scale. How was I to tell a woman I had the hots for her without crossing the line and getting the *no* word? Her words left my Toastmaster training in tatters.

I needed to respond, but what to say? I stumbled with words and fidgeted.

—I know you made that pass at me, but I was tired. I just felt like I needed sleep more than sex.

Sex. Oh my God, I said the word that ruined any couple learning about each other. She probably called it "making love" and I had to call it "sex." A pause from her. Maybe too long a pause.

—Well … I didn't see my try as that, but I thought a kiss and a close hug would have been nice.

Again, the male conquest ego had leapfrogged logic. How can sex happen without a hug or kiss first? All my muscular strength began to shrink. Her logic was outpacing my common sense. My robust arms shrunk to pretzels. I crossed them on my chest for self-protection.

My water glass was empty. I looked for something to drink. Seeing hers was half-full, I faked a choke, grabbed my neck, cleared my throat, and drank her glass dry.

—Larry, what happened?

Good God. Another question.

—I choked on that last piece of bread. It went the wrong way.

She looked at me with her eyes wide open.

—Bread? If you were choking, why did you drink something?

I felt like an actor about to exit stage and never be seen again. I guessed the truth would have to do.

—Well Marie … I like you a lot. I became scared when you made that hit on me because I didn't know if I would be able to love you. You scared the bejesus out of me.

Hoping that would resolve the issue, I desperately looked for a waitress to fill our water glasses.

Marie must have been in attack mode.

—Well, Larry, if you must know.

It was coming. Just like on the Discovery Channel show "Seconds from Disaster," she was going to bomb my hormones.

—Do you like me or what? We were good friends at the YMCA and became close friends and went to dances, but you've changed. You seem so different at times. Are you seeing someone else?

—No. I'm seeing no one but you, Marie. There are days I do feel so tired and not wanting to act like a man. That's not me, being tired.

—Maybe you're coming down with something. Have you had a physical recently?

—Physical? I'm healthier than an ox. I paused. You think it might be something physical?

—Yes. A guy like you would be hitting on me, and you've never tried.

—Well, I've had dates with other women who rejected the idea of being a target to be hit on. And I agree with them. Guys have to love to get sex, and women have to have sex to get love. Marie, can we continue this discussion later? I'm getting a headache.

She agreed. I went home, hit the sack, and slept like a newborn. The alarm wakened me. I showered, ate, and drove twelve miles to go into the details of real estate documents.

That night at the Y, I saw Marie and got a hug from her.

—Feeling better? she asked.

Faking the answer, I responded with a yes. I worked out easy, pretended another headache was starting, and left early.

My thinking about her was changing. I was a basket case. My feelings for Marie were developing to the point that I wanted to make love to her and be with her all the time, but how to express that to her without appearing overbearing? Coming on to another person too strong often hurts a relationship, yet she had made a pass at me. And she was asking questions about us and my health. I decided to go to her home.

She answered the door with a paperback in her hand.

—Hi, Larry, nice seeing you. Come on in. How are you feel—a hug with a long, slow kiss interrupted her question—ing?

My thoughts were about loving her. I could feel a very relaxed response from her as we kissed and caressed each other. She exhaled.

—Oh, please *dooo* come in.

She'd pitched her paperback on the couch were we sat. I felt it being compressed by my backside.

—I've fallen in love with you, and I wanted to say it to you.

I exploded with emotional feelings that I'd been keeping in a cage. I touched her face, caressed her cheek from ear to neck, and lightly kissed her nose.

—You mean a lot to me, and I want you.

—I want you too, Lawrence. I say your name with love all over my voice. She paused. Will you stay with me tonight? I would love to feel you next to me even if you can't do it. I just want the feel of your body giving me comfort and feeling, please?

She'd had an impact on me. Even though I might not have been able to perform, I agreed. We spent time talking on the couch and later went to her bedroom. With lights off, me in my underwear and she in a nightgown, we kissed and said goodnight. We cuddled and continued a marathon experience of kissing and touching.

When I awoke in the morning, her arm was over my chest. I hadn't felt her wrap it around me until the morning. It was wonderful. The alarm wakened her also, and we exchanged wonderful kisses. I pulled her closer to me.

—I have a love poem for you, I whispered.

Finding you in my life gives me

The feeling of seeing a flower blooming. But I will never have it better

Than your two lips on mine all day long.

She wrapped her leg over mine.

—I want you.

Our first sexual encounter left me confused. She obviously enjoyed it but never mentioned it other than as an event. My on switch went into turbo mode. We began with casual sex but with her not wanting a commitment, as I did. I asked her to move in with me with the same arrangement but again no real answer.

I decided not to push her but just to enjoy our arrangement. My urging her and myself to do something required trust in each other and in ourselves, comfort with whom we were.

We became closer, and our love sessions became more loving. My confidence in myself grew with my love for her. She became less stressed when she knew I loved her and we had a foundation for a life together. We began to talk seriously about living together and later getting married.

An event occurred that changed everything. My good friend Daniel told me that our friend Jerry was having a birthday party with a band and that if I called him, I might be invited. I called and got an invite. Marie also got a call from a friend, Peggy, telling her about her friend Jerry having a party and she should call him. She did and got her invite. We never told each other of the invites, so we didn't know we knew the same person. In addition, we didn't invite the other to go.

Imagine our shock and surprise when we saw each other at this party. We smiled, waved hellos to each other, but stayed apart for an hour. After talking with everyone but each other, it came to the point of discovery.

—I didn't know you knew Jerry, I said lamely.

—I didn't know you knew him either. Why didn't you invite me to go with you?

I was in a quandary.

We returned to her home and sat at her kitchen table. We began a real analysis of each other. Both of us stated we weren't having sex with anyone else or just dating anyone else. In addition, we didn't lie to each other; we just evaded questions about what we did or didn't do. We agreed to be honest and commit our lives to each other. Our relationship that night was complete with mutual commitments.

I gave her an engagement ring the next day. The tears in her eyes meant she agreed, and we no longer beat around the bush. We set a wedding date and mailed invitations. We agreed any prenupt parties would be rated GP.

The day of the wedding began sunny and pleasant but turned into probably the worst day ever. Nature was on our side, but humans seemed to work to undo everything.

First, the minister was not at the church. Everyone was patiently sitting in the pews. No Pastor Anderson until an elder had the brilliant idea to call his home. He had taken a nap and didn't wake up until the call.

The delay with the ceremony caused the wedding meal to be delayed. Everything had been catered—cold meat, cold mashed potatoes, and warm ice cream. Yum. Looking on the humorous side of our day, Marie and I ran to the limo for a romantic night.

Not a block away from the church, the limo stopped as it had run out of fuel. The driver had kept it idling during the two previous delays. A friend at the wedding drove us to the hotel. At last, we were at our room and wondered what would happen next.

Three's a charm. The room was too chilly, so we turned the air conditioner to a warmer temperature. Didn't work. I turned it off, and the room got too hot. Turned the air back on and it froze us. I called the front desk. It being ten o'clock at night, no service person was available, so I asked for another room.

—Sorry, we're full.

No lovemaking that night. We fitfully slept fully clothed with the air conditioning running. We later laughed at this anniversary day as a memory never to be forgotten.

I agreed with Marie to help with housework and cooking and be the outdoor barbecue chef. We felt we should be fifty-fifty with everything. We settled into a comfortable pattern of living together with a lot of laughter and few squabbles, the latter being settled by a night of passionate lovemaking. Maybe that was the reason for squabbles, to keep the fire burning.

Marie called me at the office.

—We have a problem. And I think the problem will only get bigger.

I thought she was talking about the leaking faucet we had discussed two days previously.

—Well, call your friend Anthony and get it fixed.

—No. You caused the problem.

I was getting perturbed.

—Me? What'd I do?

—You got me pregnant, and I'm so happy.

A long pause. I had lost my breath.

—Wow! We ... we're having a baby? Wow!

When I got home that afternoon, I held her all evening. I was as happy as anyone could be. Later, a sonogram determined our first child would be a boy. We started thinking of names and picked Shawn.

—Larry, get up. I have labor pains, she moaned. We have to go.

Just like our wedding day, the midnight drive to the hospital would not be good. The first snowstorm of November brought eight inches of snow and a brisk wind from the north. The weather channel advised people to stay home. The wind chill was twelve degrees. Getting our all-wheel-drive vehicle onto the road took ten minutes of back-and-forth motion in the driveway. Eight inches they said, but it looked like twenty because of drifts. We were traveling about fifteen miles per hour on the road.

Her pain was increasing. She held her belly and moaned.

—I'm kicking your ass for getting me in this condition! she screamed.

—Well kick me after you have Shawn. Just let me concentrate on getting to the hospital.

We were about a third of the way to the hospital when Marie let loose one me.

—Call an ambulance! My water broke and I'm having the baby now!

I made the call, gave them our GPS position, and stopped the vehicle. I helped her into the backseat and laid her down. Marie wailed like crazy and was in considerable pain. I helped as best I could but felt like a rookie with no education in this. The baby's head was causing dilation when a doctor arrived with the ambulance since they knew a birth was occurring. Movement of the mother wasn't possible, so the backseat became the birth table. Doctor David gave Marie local pain relief, and her pain was greatly reduced. Shawn was born at 3:13 a.m., and he and Mom were put into the ambulance and taken to the hospital. They were home in two days.

My first several times with diaper patrol were nauseating to say the least. I gagged at the smell and had to back away several times to control the desire to void my stomach. *How in the world do women do this without heaving?*

Shawn's first haircut was at home, and his baby book has a clip of his hair. The second time we went to a barber. He bawled like a calf being branded. I was holding him in the chair. That was like wrestling a greased pig. Shawn wouldn't sit still even when given a sucker. No hair was cut that day.

Marie called me several years later.

—Well, you did it again.

I considered last night's subjects but had no clue.

—What'd I do? I asked as innocently as I could.

—I'm pregnant again, and I want to thank you.

—I thought we were using birth control!

—And you conveniently forgot the condom on New Year's Eve. You remember the condition you were in then?

—Yes I do. You wanted it bad. I was bluffing; I actually recalled nothing.

—No. You were so lit I had no choice but to give it to you. I was very disappointed with not sharing your joy that night.

Feeling like a total fool, I remained silent and tried to think of a Henry Kissinger negotiation remark to put out the fire.

—I've wanted another child, and I hope you do too, Marie said.

I quickly responded truthfully.

—Yes, a second child will be a blessing. A single child should have a brother or sister.

Without Shawn really knowing why, we held his mother and my wife all evening.

We later learned a daughter was in development and decided that Tabitha Marie was a good name. She was born in September with a natural birth, no problems. Her brother, being three, didn't understand why she was so small. But he loved holding his sister and feeding her the bottle.

—When is she going to talk? he asked.

—Her cries are her talk. Talk with her and she will learn from you, Mom replied.

Shawn talked and talked to Tabitha and asked us repeatedly why she was always asleep. We said she was too young.

—But why? he would ask.

Where was Arnold Schwarzenegger when I needed him? In kindergarten, Shawn was a wreck. Mom walked with him the half mile to school the first three months. Then Shawn didn't want Mom walking with him; he had an older neighborhood friend and they walked to school. They found a shortcut to school. Later, I found out their shortcut added a quarter mile to the walk but I declined to challenge his logic.

When he was eight, he thought he knew it all. He began reading and writing and was computer literate. He wanted an ATV, computer, latte, and a cell phone. He wanted to know what a chick was. I told him a chicken. He said boobie. When Mom and I disagreed, he'd be on her side.

Tabitha turned out to be a teachers' princess. She was very articulate, always did her homework on time, and loved whiteboard cleaning. She was computer literate when her brother allowed her on the machine. When Mom and I disagreed, she'd be on my side. *Who is this Justin Bieber she likes?* She wanted an ATV, computer, latte, and a cell phone. She asked what a hunk was. Mom replied it was just a pile.

—I think it's a hot boy, she replied.

Oh, oh.

When they were eleven, both wanted a car. A convertible with a V8 engine, CD player with boom speakers, and a DVD video monitor in the roof.

—Ah, the roof of a convertible moves and has no place to hold the device, I said.

—Oh they will when we can drive, Tabitha replied.

Both children did well in high school. He played football and baseball. Tabitha was a cheerleader for football, soccer, and basketball. Both had computers, cell phones, curfews, and times they were off all communication lines.

I couldn't wait for five years for my car insurance to get lower than the property taxes. Shawn got his driver's license and within a week a speeding ticket. He has no job, so Dad paid. The car insurance went up only $75 more per month. I began to think of a second job for kid expenses. Our son became more in control with no more incidents, but I worried about Tabitha.

Shawn wanted a "sixteen-year-old" birthday party for "coming of age" complete with a band. We had to revoke the band request, but we agreed to a party with strong parental control. His friends got the band, and never had we as parents heard so much bad language that was called singing. Marie and I agreed on that and 86'd the band.

Tabitha got her driver's license. Within months, she became a better driver than her mother or me. She was involved in an accident. Someone had run a light. She was okay after the hospital visit and didn't need any additional medical care. Her car insurance remained the same.

The daughter wanted a girl's night party on her sixteenth birthday with no guys. Apprehensive, we allowed it with strict parental control for a possible panty raid. No raid. Was she an angel or what?

Our son went to college to study acting. His first play received critical acclaim. We were at the play and were awed with his skill. Shawn had never expressed an interest in high school plays.

Tabitha was eighteen and had been dating Daryl for three years. Daughter asked mother to go to the kitchen with her. Marie followed, quizzical at the request. Mom shrieked. I rushed to see what the fuss was. Marie was crying and Tabitha was looking nervous.

—Honey, what's the matter? I asked.

—Our daughter is getting married!

I asked the dread question.

—Are you pregnant?

—No, Dad. Her eyes were shedding happy tears.

—I just want this guy who proposed to me last week. I do love Daryl, and I want to be with him.

—What about college? I asked.

—I'll go. Daryl wants me to, and he'll be at the same college studying chemical engineering.

—Tabitha, please, not yet, Maria pleaded. You're too young! I like Daryl, but you haven't begun to live.

Marie and I discussed this event every day and night. We talked with Tabitha and Daryl alone and together. With reservations, we gave them our blessing. Mom and Tabitha hugged with tears in their eyes. I could not hold mine back either. My little girl was little no more.

We tried to accept the empty house. The children were taking their next steps toward maturity. Our quiet house was too quiet. We decided to enjoy life again and went on a second honeymoon to Bermuda.

There were no problems as we'd had the first time. We spent a week there enjoying pink sand beaches, fine restaurants, and dancing. We emailed friends about our new world of leisure and relaxation.

Our senior years were a time of enjoying each other and visiting friends. We traveled to many places I had been to and many she had been to and I hadn't. We looked for diamonds at a state park in Arkansas and emeralds in North Carolina. After two days of prospecting at each site, no luck, but we enjoyed the scenery.

We rafted down the river at the Grand Canyon, something new. It was a pleasant start. We were in a raft of five, but the rapids got rough, and we swamped. I lost sight of Marie and became very concerned. *Where's my wife?* Brushing past rocks, I became deathly scared for my life partner. Arising to the air after another underwater plunge, I saw her on the surface. She had been alarmed about my not staying above the water surface since we were required to wear life preservers. All the personnel reached the shore. Marie and I agreed never again.

Our travels now are on cruises, shorelines, and mountain park trails. We walk daily at home and hold hands and each other at night. We still visit the city park to see the ducks and geese and feed Daffy. We go to the Y to work up a senior sweat and recollect meeting on the exercise floor.

Time Stood Still

Time stood still for a moment. It was a clear day, in the seventies, and he was sitting on a picnic table watching Tracy on the swing in the park. They had been there about thirty minutes when a guy smoking a cigar passed Bobby.

Suddenly nothing was moving. Bobby rapidly looked around and at his watch. The seconds hand had stopped like a timer's watch. He looked around again. People looked as if they were in a photograph flash shot. A dog was running with four legs off the ground. A smiling Tracy was frozen in the swing. He saw a Frisbee just hanging there in midflight.

What's going on here? Bobby shook his head to clear his thoughts and get back on track but to no effect. *Maybe this is a dream. Could I be dreaming that I took Tracy to the park?*

Then everything moved from pause to action in the blink of an eye. Bobby tried to analyze what he had just been through. *A stroke, an aneurysm? What?* He couldn't figure it out, so he quit thinking about it.

It happened again at the grocery store the following week. He wondered why he was moving and shopping but everyone else was in a freeze frame. Bobby looked at his watch. The seconds hand wasn't moving again. The background music had also stopped. He was very conscious of his frame of mind. *Am I developing Alzheimer's?*

He deliberately dropped a can, but it froze in free fall. He freaked out. He knew he wasn't using any drugs. He started thinking his three-times-a-week greasy burger habit could have been the problem. *Why am I moving but nothing else is?*

Magically, the can fell, people began shopping again, and the music was playing.

After shopping, he went to a quiet spot at the lake park to think. There were no sudden events, no deaths or trauma in his life. *But why?*

He watched three ducks floating and bobbing and swimming as if they had no cares. He watched and wondered, *What's wrong with me?* He was entirely confused by the two timeouts in one week. *I have some disease starting at age thirty-four?* Bobby was worried and depressed. *My daughter Tracy still nine and her old man on the way to the trash heap?*

Anna and Bobby had a happy marriage until money problems became a brick wall. They separated and divorced amicably. Bobby decided that if he had Alzheimer's, he wouldn't forget Tracy, but he hoped the disease wasn't the problem. *My daughter, the love of a marriage.*

Bobby decided he needed to see a doctor or psychologist. He visited Dr. Butler and described the two time-stood-still events.

—Really? Time stopped for you and no one else, the doctor asked as he nibbled on the end of his pen as if it were a carrot.

—Yes sir. I was moving, and everything from people to dogs to machines stopped.

—How long?

—Don't know. I looked at my watch, but it was stopped. Maybe a minute or two.

—Are you having problems with sleep? Are you eating well?

—I eat and sleep well.

—Do you drink alcohol excessively or use drugs?

—Dr. Butler, I never used drugs or alcohol to excess. I like beer on weekends, but I won't take even an aspirin!

—When was your last physical?

Bobby paused as if the question had started a search of his memory's hard drive.

—Maybe seven years ago. I'm not sure.

—Are you being hypnotized to believe this stuff?

—How would I know that?

—It could happen. Is someone mad at you?

—Nope. I have a very good job. Get to visit my daughter weekly.

—Oh? You're divorced?

—Yes sir, two years now. Married, we had money issues. We had an amicable divorce. We talk often about Tracy, our daughter.

—What religious belief do you have?

—I'm a Christian.

—What religious belief did your wife have?

—Christian too.

—Are you psychosomatic?

—What's that? I can't even spell it. No. I go to bed happy, wake up hungry, hate lights at night.

—Psychosomatic. It's a mental condition in which people think they have a mental stress issue that's affecting their physical life. Do you believe in voodoo?

—No. as a Christian, devil worship is not me.

—What about a Wiccan chant?

—Again, devil worship. *Is this guy okay?*

—Could you have been given a drink or some food with a drug in it?

Bobby moved forward in his seat.

—How would I know unless I was told about it? Doctor, if that were known to me, the police would know before you did.

The doctor ignored his quick response.

—What did you eat or drink before these two incidents?

—Doc, I don't remember what I did at work two weeks ago or the news from two days ago.

—Bobby, please make a list of where you go and what food or drink you consume. This would be like a daily diary so I can assess what's going on with you. Bobby, please, this is important. You should immediately write after any activity to keep an accurate record.

Bobby agreed and did journal for several weeks, but after a while, writing crap down seemed futile since nothing was occurring, so he quit.

Then one week later, it happened at a baseball game. Two out, ninth inning, his team at bat and behind by one run. The best hitter was at bat with a three-two count. He swung just as the ball was about to enter the strike zone.

Bobby roared with the crowd. He saw the ball in the air, the bat halfway through its swing. The yells went silent. *Oh no, not again.* Bobby looked around. People were standing, their mouths open. The ballpark organ was silent. Bobby recalled having had only a hotdog and a beer that day.

As before, activity came back to life. It was a long hit, a double. But the next batter struck out, and the game was lost. Walking home, Bobby reflected on the incident and then it dawned on him. At the park, in the store, and at the ball field, he had smelled disgusting cigar smoke. *That might be the link.*

He went to Doctor Butler and explained the problem. The doctor ordered a series of tests. After testing and a long two-week analysis, time stood still for Bobby again as he learned that smoke created an allergic reaction in him that caused his memory to lapse into a hypnotic state. Bobby felt immense relief that the problem was solved. He just needed to stay away from cigar smokers.

But how? Cigar smoke could be lingering in a store, anywhere, and he could walk into it. As there was no medication for this allergy, Bobby was advised that should it occur, he should just sit and wait. He wasn't crazy. It was just his body's reaction to a chemical.

—Doctor, why am I having this problem now when for thirty-four years I've had no problem?

—Everyone has a different response. Some children are now having a severe reaction to peanut butter while others have a reaction to apples. It was believed it could be the insecticide on the apples skin that was like a poison. Bobby, you're in early midlife, but you're aging, and depending on a person's lifestyle, the body responds as best it can. I'd suggest cigarette smoke might also be a problem later in life for you.

—You mean a smoker could put me into a trance?

—No. You don't go into a trance because you continue to move. Your mind freezes on what it last saw, and your memory stays there, but your conscious state continues its movement. That's why people and sound seem to stop but your movement doesn't. It's a hypnotic freeze of what you saw, not a trance.

Not being trained in logic or mental things, Bobby shrugged and accepted the statement. He started to just smile when he saw people frozen. *They can't see what I see, but I see what they want to see.* Bobby knew it would be near impossible to stay away from cigar or cigarette smoke since it clung tightly to people's clothes for hours.

A Left Foot

Angela walked into the kitchen at the end of a long workday with so many accounting records and bills to pay. She found something on the kitchen table that wasn't supposed to be there. She figured her son must have placed it there and forgot about it. She placed it on the coffee table for him to take care of later.

But a shoe? One left shoe? What on earth? It's not his. Did a friend leave it?

—Larry, why was a left shoe on the dining table when I got home? she asked later.

—A shoe? I don't know.

—When you got home from school, was the door locked?

—Yes Mom.

—Was anything on the table when you got here?

—Only the books I was putting into my backpack. I moved everything to the couch.

—When you went out to play, you locked the door?

—Yes Mom.

She looked around the house to see if anything was disturbed. Everything was okay. It upset her, but she thought, *Oh well.*

The next day, she came home from work and spotted another left shoe on the table. She checked every window and door. Everything was fine. She grilled Larry when he came in from play.

—This is getting unnerving. Did anyone come in the house with you?

—No Mom.

Her family's safety was important. The next morning before leaving for work, she checked everything twice. She went home for lunch and checked every door and window again. No problems. She considered

Larry a responsible son who tried to follow her instructions. She felt she could trust him, but these latest events were upsetting her.

At home after work, another left shoe on the table. Angela decided her son was playing a game and would say nothing about it during supper and let him ask any leading questions. Nothing. Just general mom-son talk about school events and that night's TV viewing.

—Larry, please tell me the truth. Did a friend or anyone else borrow your key? Honey, I'm getting scared now.

—Mom, I didn't give the key to anyone. I want you safe. You're my mom, and I love you. I don't want anyone one to hurt you.

She gave him a bear hug.

The next day, the same thing. Angela was mad and getting madder with this invasion of her home. She decided to find the cause. She bought a mini camera she hid in the kitchen. It was battery operated, and any motion would turn it on. It would send a signal to the computer in her bedroom. She would finally find out what was going on.

Sure enough the next day, the camera detected motion and recorded Franky, the family dog, with a shoe in his mouth making a deposit on the table. Franky brought the shoe to the table after Larry had put his book bag on the couch. Then they went outside together.

Neighbors had no missing left shoes, so Angela could never find out what was going on. They lived in a neighborhood with no businesses nearby. And Franky was kept in a fenced backyard. *Where did Franky get those shoes? And why always a left shoe?*

Because the dog was left-handed.

That darn dog!

Senior Citizen Art of Camping

The missus and I went to her brother's home for his yearly get-together with friends. He liked to call it the Maryland Woodstock. This was his eighteenth party year. He roasted a hog and chicken, and everyone brought something to eat and drink; that was the routine. Two live bands would play after sundown for the enjoyment of the hundred guests. Many would camp on his immense property in the country and enjoy a bonfire well into the morning. They brought their families and were very friendly. They loved to talk and laugh with anyone about nearly anything. This was the annual Cascade, Frederick County, Maryland, Year Adventure.

The hog was cut into big pieces and laid out on the large barbeque grill in the morning. Chicken, hotdogs, and hamburgers were grilled later. The meal started at six o'clock in the evening. A large canopy tent covered the tables laden with other dishes, condiments, and desserts.

About thirty feet from the barbeque grill was a fenced-in chicken coop with fifteen chickens that were usually pecking for food. With the barbeque grill smoking from the pork, the chickens didn't let out a peep. They huddled, looking like a white flowing robe on a perch. They must have thought any movement or sound meant they could be going to the grill, so they were conducting themselves well.

The wife and I brought a tent to stay in overnight. We had purchased it in the spring with the intention of going to campsites at state parks, the C&O Canal sites, and even the ocean shore. We'd done this as youngsters and teenagers and knew the pleasure of hearing owls at night, an occasional other camper, and birds in the morning. Sleeping then was easy. We'd say goodnight to whomever was still awake, slip under the blankets, and drift into our dream world.

We'd set up the tent when we arrived in the early afternoon. That wasn't hard other than several matters needing major adjustments. One was placing the tent on level ground. The best ground at our site had a slight slope. We pinned down the ground pegs after we laid the tent out, stretched corner to corner. We were then supposed to run the fiberglass poles through the loops on top of the tent, but I couldn't find the loops.

We discovered we had pinned the tent down upside down. There was nothing that said This Side Up. I was the goofus. I pulled the pins and flipped the tent over. I found the instructions and read instruction one: 1. Pin to the ground right side up.

The missus tripped over a tent peg she had just hammered down during the process of setting up the second time. She fell to her knees saying something in a strange tongue. I translated.

—Go melt in a steel mill!

While we were enjoying the music after a sumptuous meal, I reflected on my early days. I'd been a Boy Scout in the fifties. I had relished the thought of getting away from home and living as Davy Crockett or Daniel Boone.

I don't mind gathering firewood, cooking for the guys, or fishing for the evening meal. That's not work; it's survival of the fittest. But working for someone else who watched you or yelled at you about getting off your butt and making some sweat and then be paid only once a week? That was probably why the war back in 1776 made sense. You could make a country out of wilderness and get away to live for yourself.

Yessiree, back then, my muscles were sore from carrying all that wood and my fingers were blistered from my hatchet. But it was an honest day's work, and I could enjoy the results later. I'd sit by the fire, my face hot and my back cold. That was the way a boy became a man.

—If half of you is hot and the other half cold, pay no attention to the cold half, my dad had told me.

My mom was a real mom. She'd tell my sisters how to cook, keep the garden tilled, and keep the house clean. My brothers and I were told while still very young that we were expected to work the fields and stay out of the house till sundown or suppertime. We worked when we had to but could fish and play baseball the rest of the time.

I grew up and got married. My work and keeping my own home meant any camping and fishing happened on weekends or vacations. I had no time to do it every day let alone play baseball. Our son and daughter wanted to do things with the missus and me on vacation, so we traveled to campsites. The kids wanted to play games on their computers and whined about their cell phones getting no signal. My God. In my day, we wrote letters and visited; we as kids wanted verbal contact.

It got near eleven thirty, our bedtime, so we went to our tent. In the morning, we had walked up the slight incline, which was an effort as we normally didn't do that. We're in our sixties, but we're not couch potatoes that watch TV from sunrise to midnight. However, we don't go dancing every weekend and get up at dawn. We worked for the man for forty-plus years and essentially wore out our bones.

That was the first time we'd used an air mattress in the tent. It was a little difficult to crawl into the tent, crawl up on the eight-inch-high air mattress, and then attempt to arrange the bedding. We'd use a flashlight to see where the blankets were and where to place our shoes. The process of removing clothes while sitting on the slippery air mattress required one of us to hold the flashlight while the other used one hand to undress, the other to stay on the mattress. After ten minutes of this, she said something I translated.

—Go follow that peg to the steel mill!

We lay down with our clothes on. I tried to become comfortable but realized I was lying on the ground. I thought we had somehow punctured the mattress. I searched for the plug and discovered we had inadvertently pulled it out during our maneuvering. So we refilled it and went through more choreography to get back into position on it. But if one of us shifted, that caused the other to do a reverse movement to counter the first. That wasn't the case with our mattress at home.

After finding comfortable positions, we entered a quiet frame of mind. Ah, the ability of humans to multitask. Our only task was sleeping, but the band was still playing, the motorcyclist beside us was seeing how high he could rev his bike, and the people on the other side were talking very loudly to be heard over the band.

And any movement caused us to slowly slide off the air mattress that was supposed to eliminate backaches from sleeping on the ground. It was quickly becoming a pain in the posterior. After an hour of slipping and pretending to sleep, we thought about going to the car, reclining the seats, and sleeping there. However, she said we wouldn't be able to lie on our sides as we usually did, and I agreed.

—Well, I guess there's only one answer. Let's tear down the tent, put everything in the car, and go home.

She agreed. We loaded up and scooted home, thirty minutes away. But we were out in the country, and it was after midnight. The turns we knew before were unfamiliar at night.

—This is Waynesboro, and west is Greencastle. Turn here, she said.

—Good.

I was yawning before we had traveled five miles.

—Well, save yourself for fifteen miles until we reach home, she said.

We discussed our adventure and what had changed over our youthful years of camping. Air mattresses were water rafts for floating on rivers and lakes. A tent in those days was only for several hours of sleep so we could go fishing and frolicking in the woods. Food was berries we picked or fish we caught. I'd heard about the Japanese eating raw fish and had tried it that way years ago. My first bite of a fish without its skin tasted like raw bread dough with a feel of stringy veggies. I spit it out.

Youth camping then was a time of not being home, living a free life with no grownups around. But we followed the rules we had learned at home because they made sense. Campfires were of a size to cook and to revel in their glow at night. Boy talk was naturally about sports and what it would be like to bicycle twenty miles to a big river and camp. Girl talk was about hot boys and John, Paul, George, and Ringo. Kids fantasized about the adventures they would have.

We reached home and went straight to the bed we knew by heart. No need to zip the tent shut, turn off the hearing aids, or wish people would quiet down. Just the pillows and the blankets on the bed speaking to us.

—Welcome!

About the Author

I have wrote for fifteen years for my family and others. That was transformed when I talked with other authors and they described the pleasure readers were having with their books. I became more intense to rewrite stories I had shared with friends to publish a book with an anthology of my stories.

I have a strong background in science, electronics and environmental recycling. In recycling, I have given many speeches to many school students and service clubs ranging from The Eagles, Rotary Clubs and Solid Waste Authorities of West Virginia.

Printed in the United States
By Bookmasters